Enamored with the Scarred Widow

A Clean Regency Romance Novel

GH00481008

Martha Barw

Benjamin Willoughby
Sophia Montgomery

Table of Contents

Prologue

December 2nd, 1814

Sophia was woken abruptly from a dream in which she had desperately been trying to escape. She was trying hard to open her eyes, knowing she must, when the pungent smell of burning reached her nostrils. It caused her to stretch out her hand across the coverlet in alarm, intending to wake Henry. Her husband, Viscount Montgomery, always slept deeply, but on this occasion, she found he wasn't there.

Sophia's heart sank as panic rose quickly within her. She stumbled out of bed and grabbed the first dress she could find inside her wardrobe.

The smell of burning was getting stronger. It was soon followed by a loud crash which sounded like something heavy had fallen over downstairs. The tendrils of smoke entering the bedchamber from under the door began to make her choke. Realising she didn't have a moment to lose, she pulled the dress on top of her nightgown, to preserve her modesty, and pushed her feet into the shoes she had discarded earlier.

She recalled that Henry had said he would be working late in his study. Whereas the light coming into the bedchamber from under the edge of the curtains, and the sound of the birds singing loudly, told her that it was dawn. Her husband must have fallen asleep at his desk. It sometimes happened, when he became too engrossed in what he was doing, that he would fall asleep before he could take the candle and come upstairs. She recalled that when she had called in on him on her way to bed that evening, he had smiled and told her to go ahead, that she shouldn't wait up for him.

Sophia pulled open the heavy oak door in her haste, crying out in pain because she had not realized how hot the brass knob had become. She was immediately met by a dense cloud of smoke, which caused her to pull her shawl across her head and lower face as she made her way blindly along the corridor. She was horrified by the sight which met her eyes when she looked down the main staircase. All she could see was a blazing inferno at the bottom of it. Nevertheless, she still put her foot on the first step, intending to go downstairs to look for Henry, when a strong hand pulled her back sharply.

She fell into the arms of the butler, Simpson, who had only been with them for a few days. She looked anxiously at him for a moment, wondering why he had taken the liberty of touching her like that. Then, she began to cry as the reality of the situation overcame her. They were trapped inside her husband's country house in Cornwall, on the edge of Bodmin Moor. The house was on fire, and she didn't know if Henry was safe.

Simpson was by this time pulling her back by the arm and shouting instructions above the roar of the fire.

"Your ladyship, please, use the backstairs. They were still intact a few minutes ago, so you should be able to get down the ground floor and then outside safely. If you could make your own way there, I shall go back to the bedchamber to rouse his lordship."

"No!" she cried in an anguished wail.

"But your ladyship, I must wake Lord Montgomery, or I cannot be responsible for the consequences," Simpson insisted.

Sophia grabbed his arm, to steady herself. "You don't understand! Henry isn't there. He was working late in his study. He must already be outside," she told him firmly. Nevertheless, even before she saw the look of comprehension on the butler's face, she knew the truth. Henry would never have left her alone in a burning building to save himself. Pushing Simpson away from her, she began to descend the main staircase, since it was the quickest way to reach the study. But before she had gone very far, she realized the fire was already raging down below and the staircase was now impassable.

The heat of the flames and the fumes quickly overcame her, and the last thing she recalled was sinking into darkness. She knew nothing more until she found herself outside, lying on the lawn by the lake. Lizzie, her lady's maid, was kneeling by her, tending to her

5

as best she could. Sophia ignored the searing pain on one side of her face and, to a lesser extent, on her hands and other parts of her body.

She said Henry's name only once before she saw the truth reflected in Lizzie's eyes.

After that, all she could recall was the sound of men shouting, the crackle of the fire, and how it hissed like an angry dragon as water from the lake was thrown on it. As the burning timber and beams fell, the air turned black and grey wit billowing ash and smoke. The servants, whose bedchambers were on the upper floor of the house or in the attic, had saved themselves by using the back staircase. When Lizzie hadn't been able to find Sophia outside, she had alerted Simpson. The butler had returned immediately to the house through the kitchen at the back after rescuing Sophia., intending to check the master's bedchamber. Simpson and the footman who had accompanied him had carried Sophia outside. The butler had miraculously only suffered superficial burns, while the footman had sustained some to his right hand when he had pulled the burning shawl from across her ladyship's face.

None of the other bedrooms on the first floor were occupied. Henry's mother, Lady Helena Montgomery, had moved from her rooms into the Dower House on the estate a few days before her son's marriage to Sophia. She professed to being most comfortable there, along with her treasured possessions and Clara, her lady's maid, who had been with her longer than she cared to remember.

After some investigation, it soon became clear that the fire must have started in the study, which had burned to the ground. Most of the other rooms and the main hall were still partially standing but were now in ruins. The majority of the family heirlooms, including many valuable family portraits and antiques, had been destroyed. Only those which Lady Helena had taken to the Dower House had survived. Fortunately, the fire hadn't reached it, nor the tenants' cottages either, for the wind had been blowing in the opposite direction.

However, the memories which steeped the house walls were all gone. The Montgomery family had lived there for centuries, and the house had been added to or changed in some way by each generation. There was nothing anyone could have done to save the old place. At least, that was what everyone told her. Nevertheless, Sophia blamed herself for not being able to save the man she loved. Every time she closed her eyes, she could still see the smouldering ruin of the home she had grown to love, even though she had only lived there for three weeks after her marriage to Henry, inside the old church in the grounds.

Sophia couldn't think of anything else, so she barely heard the quiet voice in her heart telling her that, somehow, she had to carry on. She could have sworn later that it was Henry who was speaking to her. It sounded like his voice, reminding her that none of it was her fault, that it had been down to the cruel hand of fate.

Whereas it was her destiny... to love again.

Chapter 1

The Necessity of Wearing a Veil

It was May 1816, and it had been a long winter. It was lovely to see the brightly coloured clumps of tulips in the garden again, Lady Sophia Montgomery thought as she stared from the window of her modest London townhouse. She loved to sit there, watching the passersby go about their own affairs without noticing they were being observed. She didn't recognise many of the faces walking past, since she had only bought the house in the autumn of the previous year. The plan was to be closer to Lady Helena, who lived nearby on the same street. The London Season had begun again, and the City was bustling with activity.

Sophia had noticed the familiar sense of excitement in the air outside. Debutantes were coming out for their first Season, or a later one if they hadn't been fortunate enough to have already secured a marriage proposal. Not that any of that concerned her anymore. Admittedly, she had been part of that world once upon a time when life hadn't been quite so lonely. But, at twenty-three years of age, she believed herself to be an outsider now. She considered herself still in mourning for the loss of her husband, Henry, whom she continued to love dearly. She would always have the scars on her face to remind her of his loss.

She sighed heavily, glancing around the empty parlour again, as if to check that there really wasn't anyone there with whom she could share her thoughts. When her attention returned to the garden, she took a deep breath to calm her racing heart and remind herself that she couldn't change the past, however much she wished to. She also told herself to stop blaming herself for the fire. However, deep down, she still believed that if only she hadn't fallen so deeply asleep and had instead gone downstairs to find Henry, he would have joined her then. He would be with her now.

He would not have fallen asleep at his desk in the study and knocked the candle over, which had been generally assumed was how the fire had started. She had plenty of time now to think about everything that had happened and discuss it with her mother-in-law, who tried her best to guide and help Sophia despite her own intense feelings of loss.

Almost immediately after the fire, Lady Helena had returned to the Dower House in Henry's carriage, which bore the family coat of arms emblazoned on the doors. She had received the sad news of her son's death and daughter-in-law's injury from her friends in the adjacent county of Devon, where she had been staying, once the messenger had reached them. Her old friend, the Countess of Fairfield, had insisted on accompanying her on the return journey to Cornwall. However, her kind offer had been met with a polite refusal. Lady Helena had already straightened her spine and reminded herself that she had survived the death of Henry's father. She would have to do the same now for her son, whilst supporting his young widow. It was her duty, and it was what Henry would have wanted.

Meanwhile, Simpson the butler and the housekeeper arranged for Sophia and Lizzie to be installed in the spare bedrooms at the Dower House. The servants anxiously awaited the arrival of Her Ladyship, for whom most of them had worked for many years. The doctor arrived as soon as he was called and tended to Sophia's burns. He shook his head sadly when he saw the extent of the damage to her face and estimated the size of the scar he thought she would be left with after the burns had healed. Lady Helena returned to the house to an atmosphere of stunned sorrow among the inhabitants and those who dwelled on the estate. Her son and his new wife had been held in high esteem, by both the servants and tenants on the estate farms, as well as herself.

Equally, no one knew how events would affect their own future, though not a word of their concerns was uttered by the majority, from a sense of loyalty to the family. However, there

9

were still some who whispered amongst themselves. In the end, and since Henry's father had passed away many years ago, it was left to Lady Helena to do her best to resolve matters with the help of Bates, her son's land steward. There wasn't any male relative to come to their assistance since Henry's brother, Vincent, remained estranged from the family.

Sophia continued to be distraught from time to time. Often, Lady Helena would hold her in her arms as she wept, to comfort her daughter-in-law in the only way she could. Then, for a long time, Sophia had barely spoken and merely stared unseeingly at the walls of the cottage in a worrying display of deep sorrow.

Since the estate farmland hadn't been affected by the fire, the tenants were able to retain their livelihood, at least for the time being, until a decision could be made regarding the future of the estate. Lady Helena had also done her best to find suitable positions for the servants, personally recommending them to her friends and finally managing to find employment for all of them. All except Lizzie, who stayed, for she had been with Sophia for years and was more like a friend to her. Also, Simpson the heroic butler, soon found himself another position through the agency which Henry had used to employ him.

Sophia's best friend, Lady Beatrice Stanhope, arrived as soon as she could after the tragedy, but it wasn't until early the following year since the bad weather had made the roads from Somerset impassable. She had also done her best to help Sophia stop blaming herself and recover. Both Lady Helena and Beatrice had so much more experience of life than she herself, Sophia thought, and she was very grateful to them for the kindness and consideration they showed her. Beatrice was nearly thirty years old and very happily married to James, the Earl of Stanhope. Her only regret was that so far, she hadn't managed to produce a child, and felt she was almost too old now to do so. Sophia didn't know what she would have done without the stalwart pair, or Lizzie for that matter, who never once complained about the change in her own circumstances in moving from the big house to the much smaller Dower House.

Sophia recalled how Lizzie had been so excited when they had first arrived in Cornwall from Somerset, to see the old house looming through the mist on the edge of Bodmin Moor. Henry had come with his carriage to collect them from Sophia's home, and Lizzie had whispered to her mistress that she felt just like a grand lady, travelling in such style. That was until the journey became quite exhausting, for the roads had become muddy and badly rutted, jolting them uncomfortably in their seats as the vehicle crawled along at a snail's pace.

After the fire, everyone had been so kind to Sophia. Thinking about it now, as she started out of the window, a sad smile crossed her lips. Her husband had been well liked everywhere he went, particularly by his neighbours and workers at his country seat. Many of them had come to the Dower House to pay their respects to her, even though she hadn't felt able to see anyone for a long time afterwards.

Sophia shook her head sadly. However hard she tried, she still couldn't understand why fate had intervened so cruelly in what had seemed to be their perfect life. Henry had been a good man and certainly hadn't deserved to die so young, at only twenty-six years of age. But as Lady Helena had told her many times since then, none of us knows what the future holds. In their case, not knowing had been a blessing. She comforted herself with the thought that they'd had a very short but very happy courtship and marriage before tragedy had struck. They had first met as children, then from time to time at various events as they were growing up. Across the years, it had seemed inevitable to both them and their families that they would one day become sweethearts. Her heart was broken now; of that she was in no doubt.

Sophia turned away from the window and sat down on the nearest chair. Henry had been at the heart of everything, at the centre of her life. And now, it was almost beyond her comprehension that she was facing the start of the London Season.

But this time she was without her own dear mama, who had passed away four years ago, and Papa had been gone even longer. The thought of what she faced made her utterly miserable.

What on earth am I doing here in London, especially during the Season?

The Season was a time for laughter and fun, and the thrill of finding an eligible bachelor, one whom you wished with all your heart would turn into a suitor. It was a time for endless talk of new gowns and Paris fashions and the latest hair ornaments with your own dear mama and friends. She appreciated that Lady Helena and Beatrice had been trying hard to persuade her to move forward with her own life so that she could find happiness again, but she just knew that would never happen.

I do not belong here.

She traced her finger along the jagged scar on the right-hand side of her face which ran from her temple to the middle of her cheek, then from there down to her neck. How would she carry on without Henry, and with this dreadful scar, which was a constant reminder of the night that had changed everything? If only she could turn back the clock, but that was impossible, of course, however much she wished for it.

Fishing out her hanky, she wiped the tears away from her eyes, telling herself that she must accept the way things were. Henry was gone, and she was still here, without him. She could remember her father saying quite clearly after Grandmama had passed away that life was for the living. As difficult as it was to accept, she knew she was going to have to try to take that to heart from now on.

Not knowing what else to do or how to begin changing her own circumstances, she stood up again to stare at the street outside. She tried to imagine herself being part of the throng of people hurrying past— because she also had somewhere to go. Maybe it would help her to recover if she started going out again.

12

There would be plenty going on, once the Season was in full swing. She would need to choose where she went carefully, as some of the places still wouldn't be appropriate for her. She was no longer a debutante wearing a white gown, but a widow dressed from head to foot in black, who had never once imagined that at twenty-three years of age she would be mourning the loss of her much-loved husband. She would never be able to understand why life had to be so cruel.

As she withdrew her hand from her face, quite by chance, she noticed the paint brushes and canvas which had been long forgotten sitting on the table next to the wall. She had always been able to lose herself in her art in the past, but since the fire, her inspiration had completely disappeared. She no longer knew how or what to paint. However, all of a sudden, as she continued to look at her old painting paraphernalia, she knew she couldn't carry on as she was any longer. She felt suffocated and overwhelmed by life.

The clock on the wall struck midday, pulling her from her gloomy thoughts. Sophia became conscious that it was a beautiful spring day outside, with the sun shining brightly. She decided that it was far too nice to still be stuck indoors, feeling sorry for herself, knowing it wasn't possible to change the past and that pretending it was would only lead to further heartache.

Sophia suddenly became determined to reclaim some semblance of her former life. After closely examining her paintbox and brushes, she realised that there was absolutely no reason why she shouldn't pay a visit to the Royal Academy of Arts to look at the paintings. It was a perfectly respectable thing for a widow in mourning to do. She had been there in the past, with only her maid for company, and it would soothe her to be amongst the fine works of art on display. As a quiet excitement began to overcome her, Sophia wondered if she might not also gain some inspiration from the visit. She dared to imagine being able to paint again after seeing the work of the famous artists on display, many of whom she knew had had their own troubles to bear.

To stop herself from changing her mind, Sophia quickly instructed Soames, the butler, to have her carriage made ready. Whilst Lizzie, also excited by the thought of an outing, helped her dress appropriately in one of the black gowns Sophia wore when she did occasionally leave the house. It was quite plain, without any ornamentation. Lastly, and most importantly, Lizzie carefully helped her put the black veil over her face which Sophia never left the house without. Wearing it prevented the ladies of the ton from scrutinising her scarred and disfigured skin and therefore reduced the possibility of her overhearing them talking about it afterwards. Such things distressed her and destroyed any fragile confidence she had managed to rebuild.

Once the pain from the injury had lessened, she had become used to the reaction of others if she didn't wear a veil in public. She had not so far been able to completely get beyond the shame she felt in revealing her face to strangers, who had no idea how it she had gotten her scar. Whilst she had never thought of herself as exactly beautiful—something Henry had always gallantly insisted she was—she had at least believed her features were satisfactory.

A short while later, Sophia and Lizzie left the carriage and stepped inside the Royal Academy of Arts. As they walked through its corridors and hallowed halls, Sophia allowed herself to become lost in the beauty of the paintings on the walls around her.

They finally reached a gallery which she hadn't visited before which appeared to be empty. Sophia's attention was immediately caught by a particularly striking landscape hanging on the wall opposite entrance. Finding its rolling hills and lush countryside too captivating to simply pass by, she stopped directly in front of it, unable to take her eyes from the canvas. While Lizzie sat on a nearby bench to rest, Sophia's curiosity and fascination soon overcame any self-consciousness she might usually have felt. So, without even glancing around to make sure no one else had come in, she gently lifted the veil from her face so she could see the painting better.

Oblivious of all else, she indulged in her pressing need to inspect the brush strokes and discover how the artist had achieved such depths of colour. She smiled to herself, recalling how, when she had only just started to paint, she had believed there was just one shade of green. It was Henry who suggested that she examine the leaves, grass, flowers, and foliage in the garden more closely to test her hypothesis. And he had been right to do so. She had quickly realized that Nature had an entirely different view on the matter of green and corrected herself accordingly.

What will I do now, she wondered, without him to guide me? She still didn't know the answer to that question, but she believed the little voice she had heard speaking to her in the weeks after the fire was right: Somehow, she needed to carry on. With that in mind, she continued admiring the landscape until she felt a sense of hope stirring somewhere deep within her again.

Chapter 2

A Passion for Art

The gentlemen's club near The Strand was one of Lord Benjamin Willoughby's favourite places in London. He had known his friend Robert since childhood, and they often met there. They would often enjoy a coffee together while reading the newspapers, discussing whatever came to mind at the time. That morning, however, it wasn't long before Robert could see that Benjamin was preoccupied and asked him what was bothering him.

Despite knowing his friend very well, Benjamin was embarrassed to tell the truth at first. He did not wish to air his domestic troubles with his friend or appear to be complaining and spoil their coffee. Nevertheless, Robert was clearly waiting for a reply.

"It's hardly worth mentioning, since it's the same old story. I had an argument with my mother last night. I find it difficult to believe sometimes just how relentless she can be in her quest to see me married off to a woman of what she calls 'impeccable lineage.' Not forgetting that she must also, of course, be a great beauty." Benjamin attempted to grin before drinking another mouthful of coffee and then sighing heavily. He found himself quite unable to keep up the pretence any longer that Lady Rosamund Willoughby's behaviour on the previous evening hadn't affected him.

"She simply can't see what the problem is and refuses to understand how it appears to me when all of the marriages in my family have been arranged. As a result, she takes the view that what she is doing in trying to press me into a marriage of convenience is perfectly acceptable. It's unlikely I shall be wealthy enough to match the circumstances of the woman of my mother's choice, but she will be gaining a husband, which, for some unknown reason, is apparently what she desires from the bargain. Whereas I regard it all as highly unacceptable and appalling, however I look at it," he elaborated, feeling slightly uncomfortable at his outburst, given that he hadn't intended to express his feelings quite so strongly.

As Robert was looking thoughtful and didn't appear to be about to reply, Benjamin continued.

"I would also say that, irrespective of her persistence, I really don't believe that such an arrangement will suit me. Especially when I wish more than anything else to be happily married for the majority of my days on this earth. I simply don't see how that will be possible without me first having a deep connection to the woman I marry. I don't want some superficial arrangement with one of this Season's latest debutantes, who will more than likely not have a mind of her own. Or will be unable to think of anything other than gowns and bonnets. At the same time, I don't fancy being hotly pursued by another one of those dreadful mamas who are as relentless and persistent as the one I already have. It all seems like far too much to ask," Benjamin finished, bristling with indignance.

Robert was by this time nodding sympathetically. He completely understood how his friend felt. Having been fortunate to marry for love the previous year, he was feeling a little guilty, for as yet, he hadn't been able to come up with a plan to extract Benjamin from the predicament he was in. In comparison to his friend's, his own life was perfect in ways he had never dreamed possible. He loved his wife dearly, and she him. So much so that neither of them could imagine life without the other.

In an attempt to restore their previous good humour, Benjamin turned the conversation back to politics and began to raise counterarguments to the views on universal suffrage that Robert had expressed earlier. After the two men had thoroughly explored the topic and finished their excellent coffee, Robert asked to be excused; he had an important business matter to oversee. Benjamin pretended his good mood was restored and bid Robert a cheerful adieu. However, as soon as Robert had walked through the door and there was no longer any chance of him turning around to look behind him, Benjamin's smile fell away, he leaned

17

his chin on his hand and reverted to his former dark train of thought.

After sitting there lost in thought and refusing the waiter's offer of another cup of coffee, or possibly a different newspaper, Benjamin left the club. On the spur of the moment, since he was passing by the august building, he decided to pay a visit to the Royal Academy of Arts. He entered and began wandering aimlessly through the many corridors and galleries, trying his best to take an interest in the latest exhibition, but without a great deal of success. In truth, his thoughts were still focused on the disagreement he'd had with his mother earlier about his marriage prospects. Being involved in arguments or disputes with others wasn't at all like him, so he found the current one particularly upsetting. Especially since it concerned his mother, whom he held in high regard.

Sighing deeply, he persuaded himself to return to the present and at least try to enjoy being surrounded by the most spectacular and stunning art currently in London. He had been an avid patron of the arts for several years on a modest scale. He prided himself on being always on the lookout for new and talented painters who might be encouraged in some way by his support. The intention was that his support should place them in a position where they could achieve greater acclaim, followed by success. Benjamin also knew the majority of the prominent figures in the art world, with whom he was on first name terms. What still amazed him was to see how a gifted artist could develop across the years, heightening their skills as they worked. Creating so much beauty to release into the world and add to that which already existed seemed a minor miracle to him.

However, despite his efforts to put it aside, the argument with his mother popped into his thoughts again. Although he had tried earlier to make light of it when talking to Robert, it had been a particularly harsh one. His mother had been very angry that he had refused once again to accept her help in finding a wife, and she had resorted to making a number of bitter accusations, all of which, in his opinion, were completely untrue. His mother had finished her diatribe with the wounding remark that he was deliberately behaving badly by not doing as she asked simply because he no longer cared for her. She had become tearful after that and announced she felt faint. Naturally, Benjamin had felt responsible for her ill turn because of upsetting her so badly. Whilst the truth of the matter was, though it pained him to think he was being unkind to his mother, he knew he would feel a whole lot worse if he agreed to do as she wished and pursue a romance which his heart wasn't in.

Unable to see a resolution to their differences, he had been desperately hoping to find solace in his visit to the Academy. He had believed that he would be able to lose himself in the beauty of the paintings, escaping the pressures of life, even if just for a short time. If only his mother understood that he knew how to appreciate a lot of different forms of beauty in the world. His enjoyment of it didn't need to solely revolve around having a pretty, vacuous debutante on his arm. Nor would it necessarily be true, as she argued it would, that his life would be complete once he was successfully matched and then married well. Of course, he was well aware that it was the opinion of the ton. Essentially all that mattered to them was that his bride should be from one of the oldest families in the land and look absolutely stunning. Whereas however hard Benjamin tried to change his view of the matter to please his mother—and he desperately wished not to continue hurting her—as far as he was concerned, the ton's expectation of him was unrealistic. Moreover, it had become a burden which weighed far too heavily on his shoulders.

As he entered one of the side rooms at the Academy which he couldn't recall visiting for some time, he was surprised to see a woman standing perfectly still in front of a large landscape painting. She appeared to be mesmerised by it. Her tall, slender figure, and chestnut-brown hair also caught his attention. She appeared to be accompanied by her maid, who was seated on a bench nearby, looking bored. Following the lady's example, he took a leisurely moment to admire the landscape painting. It was indeed stunningly beautiful, and Benjamin soon appreciated the depth of mood captured by the brushstrokes and the kaleidoscope of green tints the artist had used to create his effects. The skill in execution it was truly astounding, but Benjamin could not see the name of the painter.

Not wishing to stare too long at the painting or the woman and risk intruding on her thoughts, he couldn't help wondering if she shared his passion for art.

Chapter 3

A Visit To The Royal Academy

As Sophia examined the intricate details of the landscape, apparently painted by an unknown artist, more closely, she began to suspect it had been painted by Mr John Constable. She lifted her veil to see better and was suddenly transported by the artist's skilful use of colour and light to a different place in her memory. In the painting, an old shepherd and his dog were walking across the land behind a flock of sheep. The scene took her back to a day she had spent with Henry on his estate in Cornwall not long after their marriage. They had left the grounds of the big house and taken a walk across the farmland nearby. There, she had seen a flock of sheep under a pale winter sky and decided to paint the scene later. But she never had.

Coming back to the sheep in the landscape, she observed that they must have been painted later in the year. And if the artist was indeed Mr Constable, it had more than likely been done in Suffolk, his favourite background. The vibrancy of blue in the sky made the canvas come to life for Sophia, and she fancied the land below was being watched over by a celestial being gazing down from the cerulean sky. *It truly is an inspiration!*

Her mind began to wander idly through the palette of colours she might use in her new painting, and how she might mix different ones to get the exact shades she wanted. Unfortunately, despite her absorption, the rustic scene reminded her too much of Henry and their happy life on the estate, and a wave of familiar melancholy swept over her. Not only did she miss Henry but also those all too few carefree days they had spent together in the country. With him by her side, sharing her love of Nature, wandering through fields and valleys, she had felt truly inspired.

Back in the gallery, she was suddenly seized by the urge to hurry home and try her best to recapture the essence of those special moments spent with Henry on canvas, in the same way as the unknown artist had in the landscape. It also came to her with a start that she was feeling the same as she used to when a flicker of inspiration ignited within her which she knew she couldn't ignore. It compelled her to finally turn away from the painting, for the ache in her heart became unbearable under the weight of bittersweet memories.

Quite unexpectedly, however, and without knowing why she had assumed she was alone, Sophia caught sight of a man standing nearby. He seemed to be in his late twenties, tall, with broad shoulders, and dark hair. Before she had time to form any sort of opinion of him, she realised to her dismay that he was not looking at the painting at all. Instead, he was gazing fixedly at her face, which, she suddenly remembered with a start, was no longer hidden by the veil. Sophia immediately felt anxious and put her hand up to touch the scar. She didn't know this man, so she was a little afraid of him. Why was he still looking at her like that? It was her scar, of course.

It came almost simultaneously to her mind that it wasn't proper for a stranger to see her face in such close proximity, and it was certainly rude of him to stare like that. Flustered, she lowered her veil, wondering why on earth she had been so foolish as to come there that day.

Feeling uncomfortably self-conscious, she looked quickly away from the man, who seemed to remember his manners and averted his eyes. Clearly, she thought, he had realised she had caught him staring at her. Lifting her chin in silent rebuke, Sophia made a beeline for Lizzie, feeling much safer with her maid at her side. They exchanged a few words and exited the gallery, leaving the man alone as they made their way out of the Academy and headed for the carriage to take them home.

However, as the carriage rattled its way along the streets to the townhouse, Sophia couldn't help thinking about the stranger. Even though she believed she ought not to, she felt curious about him. In fact, the entire afternoon had left her with mixed feelings. Eventually she recalled, much to her surprise, that when she had focused her attention on the stranger instead of her own insecurities, there had been warmth in his gaze. He'd had the nicest hazel eyes and was really quite handsome. The thought brought a blush to her cheeks, which hadn't happened for a long time. Secretly, she felt more than a little ashamed of herself for thinking such things.

However, once she was safely home again, she successfully dismissed him from her mind. Sitting in the drawing room at the front of the house, she became fully absorbed in examining her paints and brushes and planning her painting in earnest. The light in the drawing room was good, much better than in the parlour at the back of the house. Lizzie had also helped her change into the old dress she hadn't worn for a long time. It was the one she always used to wear when she painted. Her justification for choosing it was that it didn't matter if it soon became covered in more spots of paint, which would only add to those which were already daubed on it. Although it was a dark dress, apart of course from the paint, it wasn't black but more of a purplish shade. Lizzie had remarked upon this, and how nice Sophia looked in it. The maid was delighted to be able to think this might lead to a new beginning for her mistress, who would eventually stop wearing mourning clothes.

Sophia didn't respond. She was already feeling far too self-conscious in the purple dress, and more than a little guilty. She was still mourning the loss of her husband, she chided herself. Not only had she chosen to wear a purple dress instead of her usual black one, but she had also been thinking about a stranger, whom she thought quite handsome and had nice eyes. Even worse, he had seen her scar. All of it is highly improper, she thought. As the hot

23

blush returned to her cheeks, she was very glad that Lizzie couldn't read her mind.

It felt strange to be wearing the dress again and seeing the spots of colour already daubed on the skirt from her earlier work, which Henry had teased her about. He had asked if she wished to turn herself into a painting then more seriously reminded her that if that was the case, there was no need—she was already beautiful enough. When she had questioned his statement, not believing him, he had said that it was his view of her, and she would never persuade him otherwise.

A tear slid down Sophia's cheek at the memory. She slowly brushed it away with the lace handkerchief she pulled from her pocket. She was unwilling to release the memory of that day so soon, for it was the first time she had recalled it since Henry's death. She did not wish it to slip naturally away by itself. But at the same time, she tried to hold onto her earlier determination when admiring the landscape at the gallery, telling herself that it really was time for her to paint again.

She began, hesitantly at first, to sketch her ideas for a new canvas. It was to be similar in theme to the landscape, but her scene would be instilled with the memories she still had of that wonderful day out walking with Henry. Exercising her memory, she was gradually able to recall it in more detail.

She carried on until her pencil was moving across the page more confidently, and she soon became fully absorbed in what she was doing. It wasn't long, however, before Soames came into the drawing room, followed by Lady Helena. Despite the interruption, Sophia was delighted to see her mother-in-law, wondering what she would make of her painting again.

In addition, Lady Helena had encouraged her to come out of mourning, especially after Sophia had insisted on wearing widow's weeds for far longer than she needed to. Lady Helena had said that she believed Henry would not have expected this of Sophia. She said that knowing her son as well as she did, she was sure he would only have wanted Sophia to find happiness again. Her assertion had implied that she would be unlikely to find it in such drab attire.

After greeting Sophia with a kiss on the cheek, Lady Helena glanced with obvious surprise first at the dress Sophia was wearing and second, at the canvas in front of her, where the initial outlines were appearing.

"How wonderful to see you painting again, dear," she said, though she clearly thought it wise not to comment on the dress. She knew Sophia would tell her about the change as soon as she was ready. Whilst Lady Helena sincerely hoped her daughter-in-law would start wearing more colourful clothes again, believing they matched her personality and would encourage a return to her previously cheerful disposition. In her opinion, that was long overdue.

Sophia returned Lady Helena's kind comment with a half-smile, trying not to feel guilty because of how much she was enjoying herself. As a means of diverting her mother-in-law's attention from the canvas, she announced that she had been about to stop for a while to rest and invited Lady Helena to have tea with her. That way, she said, they could share any news they might have.

The two women sat comfortably side by side on the settee, as the housemaid served them with tea from bone china cups and the daintiest slices of cake Lady Helena declared she had ever seen. She tried to avert her eyes from her daughter-in-law's unfortunate scar, which did its best to spoil her otherwise beautiful face. Although she hadn't admitted it to Sophia, she approved of her decision to wear a veil, at least until she was feeling stronger. The ladies of the ton could be extremely cruel, and her daughter-in-law was the very last person in the world to deserve this. A more kind-hearted and gentle person it would be impossible to find, and she had been delighted when Henry announced their betrothal.

Lady Helena's eyes filled momentarily with tears before she managed to blink them away and keep them hidden. She took another bite of Cook's very tasty sponge cake. She hoped with all her heart that Sophia would find another suitor before long, and that he would be able to ignore her obvious disfigurement in the light of her charming, and beautiful disposition.

Chapter 4

Benjamin and Lady Charlotte Sinclair

Later that afternoon, Benjamin's valet helped him get dressed for a dinner which was being hosted by his mother, Lady Rosamund Willoughby. As Hugh skilfully finished tying his grey silk cravat, which complimented the blue waistcoat which he had already put on, Benjamin could feel his heart sinking. Now that he was almost ready to go downstairs again, he was well aware that this would be another good opportunity for his mother to act as his matchmaker.

It had reached the point where he felt as if he didn't have the right to voice any opinion whatsoever regarding his future. It was almost as if he only mattered to his mother in relation to her getting her own way. The irony of the situation was that she seemed to think the opposite was true. It made him exceedingly grateful for the trust fund his father had set up for him, which allowed him to some degree to live as he chose. Without it, he would have been much more under his brother's control, since as the eldest son, Simon had inherited their father's vast fortune. And Simon was still inclined to comply with Lady Rosamund's wishes despite him being a grown man who should by now have cultivated an opinion of his own.

Just then, however, an image of the woman Benjamin had seen earlier at the Royal Academy came unexpectedly into his thoughts. However strange it might seem, he couldn't seem to forget her, nor help wondering who she was. The way she had been staring at the landscape, seemingly scrutinising every minute detail of it, was intriguing. He smiled to himself when he realised that thinking about her also helped him keep his mind off his own troubles, albeit for very short interludes. Shrugging his shoulders in an attempt to get himself in the right frame of mind for what lay ahead, he glanced briefly in the looking glass before walking the short distance to the door of his bedchamber. It was equally pointless to continue thinking about the woman at the Academy he supposed, but with no small amount of regret.

The family townhouse in London which his father had purchased several years ago, again at his mother's instigation, was considerably larger and grander than his own. It didn't take him long to reach it, so only a short while later, he was being greeted cheerfully enough by Frobisher, Lady Rosamund's long-suffering butler. Frobisher escorted him along the opulent hall to the drawing room, where his mother had been impatiently awaiting his arrival. She was clearly in a state of excitement. After he had only just walked through the door and she had barely greeted him, she was unable to keep the reason for it to herself any longer. She quickly pulled Benjamin by the arm so that he had no choice other than to sit down next to her on the settee when he would have preferred one of the chairs which accommodated his size much more comfortably. Barely waiting long enough for him to sit down and stretch out his long legs in front of him, his mother told him that she had someone very special whom she would like him to meet.

Much to his dismay and surprise, as soon as he followed her line of sight, he noticed for the first time that they weren't alone. A young lady was seated demurely on a chair set against the far wall, with her eyes lowered, presumably waiting to be formally introduced to him. He had been so overwhelmed by the attention from his mother and the intensity of her welcome that he had only been looking at her, not the rest of the room. He wondered why his mother had asked him to sit beside her when he ought to have approached the other occupant of the room immediately for an introduction, whether or not he wished for one. It seemed that Lady Rosamund's behaviour was also now having a detrimental effect on her manners, for it appeared she was starting to forget them!

Benjamin quickly stood up again and waited for his mother to continue speaking. However, the displeasure he felt at such an obvious display of matchmaking stretched his kind, tolerant nature to its boundaries. So much so, the smile he usually wore, which came from an optimistic and cheerful disposition, turned immediately into a scowl without any intention on his part.

Benjamin also couldn't help looking at his mother angrily. It had clearly become impossible for her to desist from behaving like this. It certainly wasn't in the least amusing or acceptable when he had expressed his own wishes on the matter. Why couldn't she acknowledge that he was a fully grown man and the master of his own destiny? If she would only open her eyes and look at him standing in front of her, she surely couldn't fail to see it.

But judging by the look on her face, she instead believed he had mislaid any common sense he once upon a time might have possessed. This was especially concerning his ridiculous refusal to be guided by her in matters of the heart. She had told him many times before that she only wished most generously to share with him what she regarded as her wealth of experience of the world. He undoubtedly knew what was going through her mind again at that specific moment.

In addition, Lady Rosamund felt antagonised by the fact that her youngest son clearly took her for as a fool. A fool was something Lady Rosamund Willoughby knew she certainly was not, especially when she ranked as highly as she knew she did in the estimation and regard of the ladies of the ton. Surely, Benjamin must realise that she would only introduce him to the most suitable young ladies?

As a result, she carried on regardless of what she perceived to be Benjamin's appallingly bad manners, hoping it wouldn't spoil his chances on this occasion. She went ahead with her plan to introduce him to Lady Charlotte Sinclair, a young heiress whose beauty and charm were undeniable. Again, this was in the opinion of the ladies of the ton, which Lady Rosamund considered to be an impeccable recommendation for her as a future daughter-in-law. It was also a considerable advantage that she was extremely wealthy, came from a well-respected family, and had an impeccable lineage.

Nevertheless, although Benjamin exchanged the usual pleasantries with Lady Charlotte, as his mother and polite society expected of him, he was unable to prevent the scowl from returning to his face every time he managed to remove it. He appeared to both ladies, therefore, to be of a somewhat fierce disposition, when that wasn't his true nature at all. Also, he appeared to have little to say beyond what the rules of civility required of him, again, unlike him. He had no wish whatsoever to encourage either his mother or Lady Charlotte Sinclair into believing he was considering the young lady as wifely material, since she could only be regarded by him as a complete stranger. Conversely, he also knew that his mother would be hoping for him to propose marriage right away, just in case another gentleman decided to beat him to it!

As a result, it was a relief for all of them when Frobisher announced that dinner was about to be served. Benjamin was informed then by his mother, speaking in a stage whisper, that she had partnered him with Charlotte at the dinner table. At that, her guest blushed quite prettily, Lady Rosamund though. Whereas Benjamin fervently wished he could return home immediately, to hide behind the closed door of his study.

Despite her obvious beauty, he had no interest whatsoever in Lady Charlotte Sinclair. He wished he could at least to announce it to someone who would believe it.

However, glancing at Lady Charlotte's face made Benjamin feel that he may well have been exceedingly unkind to her in failing to meet her expectations of him, which it was equally not in his nature to do. From talking to Lady Charlotte, he was well aware that, like his mother, she had also been trying her best to cultivate the beginning of a romance with him. This all caused Benjamin to groan to himself over what he experienced as considerable misery.

The situation didn't get any better as the evening progressed. During dinner, and under Rosamund's ever watchful eye, he was obliged to continue to struggle to converse with Lady Charlotte. Despite not usually being at a loss for words, Benjamin found himself becoming tongue tied, unable to string those the words he did manage to utter into the right order to form a sentence.

The more dismayed he became by it, the worse the affliction grew. His inability to speak properly appeared to delight his mother, though, and he realised that she clearly incorrectly attributed it to him being captivated by Lady Sinclair's stunning appearance and overwhelmed by her charm.

Benjamin's thoughts returned eventually to the veiled woman he had encountered at the Royal Academy. He found it impossible not to think of her and the temporary feeling of peace it gave him from the predicament he was in. Despite Lady Rosamund continuing to give him encouraging looks throughout dinner, he tried his best to ignore them. However, by pudding, he noticed she had changed her mind about his trouble speaking, and since he was not gazing adoringly into Lady Charlotte's eyes, had reverted to her earlier opinion that he really was insufferable.

Now even more anxious and unsettled because of his mother's scrutiny, Benjamin had to desist altogether from trying to converse with Lady Charlotte. He simply did not believe it was right to make any young lady wrongly believe that he had a romantic interest in her when he quite simply didn't. Doing so was the height of extremely bad manners and ungentlemanly behaviour, in his own humble opinion.

He could easily imagine the outlandish thoughts which must be going through his mother's head by then; she would no doubt have already gone beyond envisioning a courtship between Lady Charlotte and himself and already had them married off. Possibly, he thought with horror, she had even calculated the requisite number of grandchildren she could expect from such a match.

The whole thing is was insufferable, Benjamin thought, resorting to the safety of silence. Unable to wait for dinner to end, he finally breathed a sigh of relief when it was time for Simon, at the head of the table, to put him out of his misery. Simon stood up from the dinner table and invited the gentlemen to join him in the parlour for drinks. However, with the benefit of hindsight, Benjamin should have realised that he still wouldn't get any peace from his mother's unwanted attentions. Even while he was sipping his wine, it soon became obvious to him that she had spoken to Simon beforehand and persuaded him to exert his influence on his younger brother. As a result, Simon took up the pursuit where Rosamund had been obliged to leave it.

Not even making any of the usual remarks about the food at dinner, the vintage of the wine, or what had occurred at his club that day, Simon immediately launched into a conversation which began with an observation on how well Mama had excelled herself on this occasion. Moreover, he added, Benjamin would be a fool not to consider taking Charlotte as a wife. Despite her obvious physical attractions, she was extremely wealthy and, for some unknown reason, had seemed to show a considerable amount of interest in Benjamin during dinner. Simon had tried to make light of it, clapping him good naturedly on the back when he said all this, but Benjamin remained firmly unconvinced.

All Simon had succeeded in doing was to remind him again of the high expectations set by his family and that they believed beyond the shadow of a doubt that success in life had money at its heart. Not kindness or compassion, and certainly not love! They completely ignored the attributes which Benjamin strongly believed one should cultivate, and which the woman he married should most certainly possess.

Chapter 5

A Change of Circumstances for Sophia

Two days later, Sophia met her late husband's lawyer, Mr Josiah Blackwood, in the study at her townhouse. She had recently received a letter from him requesting a meeting, to discuss the management of her financial interests. She could have met him at his offices in the Strand, but as he had offered to come to her, and she felt more comfortable seeing him in a less formal environment. So, she had sent a letter by return, agreeing to the appointment and thanking him for his consideration. Although neither of them ever thought it would happen, Henry had told her that she would have nothing to worry about financially in the event of him dying before her. His affairs were in good order, he had said, and his will had been written by Mr Blackwood in such a way that it made certain she would be well taken care of for the rest of her life. He had also bequeathed his title and interests in the family estate to his estranged brother Vincent. This had been expected by both Lady Helena and Vincent, regardless of the estrangement, which had occurred some years ago in a disagreement with his father.

Sophia had only met Henry's lawyer on one other occasion, just before they were married. She had gone with him to Mr Blackwood's office so that he could sign some papers and wished to take her shopping afterwards. She hadn't found the experience a particularly comfortable one, being in awe of the lawyer and his environment, also secretly feeling there was something about him which wasn't quite right. Although he spoke politely enough to her, she was left with the distinct impression that he was a formidable man in both manner and dress. However, it wasn't for her to criticise him or doubt Henry's judgement.

Nevertheless, not long after Mr Blackwood had arrived at the townhouse, she couldn't help feeling even more uneasy when he began to go through the various ledgers he had brought with him. He muttered to himself as he did so, frowning at the figures written within them. Not understanding why the things he insisted upon were necessary, Sophia began to feel somewhat alarmed. The situation didn't get any better when he presented her with the distressing news that her finances were not, as she might have expected, in a favourable state. That was when she knew for certain that something wasn't right.

Sophia's stomach began churning uncomfortably, and she started to feel a little faint. She put off asking Lizzie to get her a glass of water from the kitchen as she didn't want to make a fuss. It was also once again a warm morning, so it was quite hot under the veil she had decided to wear. She wished she could run outside and sit quietly under the shade of the old apple tree. She desperately wanted to pull off the veil, for she felt almost as if she were suffocating.

Nevertheless, leaving Mr Blackwood at that point was impossible, so she tried instead to gather her thoughts and continue to converse with the gentleman in whom Henry had placed so much trust. Tentatively, she asked him the one or two questions she was capable of, in an attempt to clarify the matter. But she hardly heard his responses, for her mind was already whirring with the implications of the shocking news and how it had come to pass. Henry assurances that all would be well rang in her head, and it seemed inconceivable that he could have let her down in such a way.

Mr Josiah Blackwood however began to shake his head and looked at her sadly as he went on to reveal a few meagre details of how she had been put in such a difficult position. He told her that the losses which had been incurred as a result of the fire, combined with several unwise investments by her late husband, had resulted in her being left in a highly precarious position.

Feeling completely stunned and still unable to believe that her finances weren't in perfect order, Sophia was naturally in quite a state when Mr Blackwood took his leave. Not knowing or understanding the full extent of the problem, she feared the worst, thinking she would very soon be penniless. Consequently, as soon as the lawyer had left the house, she began to sob uncontrollably. She was discovered a short while later by Lady Helena, who was extremely concerned to find her daughter-in-law in such a state, and she immediately wished to know the reason for it. In truth, she expected Sophia to say, as she usually did, that her tears were for Henry and how much she still missed him.

Consequently, Lady Helena was very surprised when Sophia told her instead about the lawyer's visit and Mr Blackwood's opinion that she could expect a reduction in her circumstances. The most alarming factor in Lady Helena's view was that Sophia didn't really know how all of this had come about.

"I have to say, I find this very hard to believe, Sophia. Especially knowing how particular Henry was about his finances. While never showing any signs of meanness, he was careful with money and he most certainly loved you dearly," she said, looking troubled as she held her daughter-in-law's hand. "I know this is the last thing in the world my son would have wished to happen, so there must be some mistake. Henry would have regarded it as a complete disgrace to have the threat of the debtors' prison hanging over him, and it is totally inconceivable. I am certain he would have taken every precaution against something like this happening."

Lady Helena paused, deeply troubled by the turn of events. This truly was the very last thing she had expected or would have wished for Sophia. Her life was hard enough as it was, losing Henry and being left with that dreadful scar. Whilst the threat of becoming destitute would be in itself quite unbearable for any young woman to countenance, bringing with it the very real risk of poverty if she couldn't find employment as a lady's companion, governess, or otherwise. However, Lady Helena was not prepared for that to happen to Sophia. Thankfully, she had sufficient money of her own to be able to care for her if need be.

Thinking quickly, she said, "If you don't mind me saying so, my dear, I believe that we need to arrange another meeting with Mr Blackwood as a matter of urgency, to find out exactly where all of Henry's, and now your, money, has gone! All of this is most odd, and in my mind, highly irregular!"

Chapter 6

Matters Of The Heart

Meanwhile Benjamin was attending a lecture on the history of art at a venue near the Minerva Press in Leadenhall Street. Through one of the circulating libraries he subscribed to, and in particular the Press, he had become interested in reading gothic novels. The lecture room wasn't one he usually frequented, but he was enjoying what was being said about his favourite painter, William Turner.

That was until he began thinking again about what had happened last night, and how badly his mother and brother had behaved. It had to be said, it had been even worse than usual! Admittedly, Lady Charlotte was very beautiful and extremely wealthy with it, which would be more than enough for a lot of the gentlemen he knew to recommend her as a good catch. But not for him. Even after he had slept on his dilemma once again, the fact remained that Lord Benjamin Willoughby was his own man, and it simply wasn't within him to pursue a romance with a lady for those reasons alone.

How on earth was he to begin it when he didn't even feel any sort of spark between them? That was apparent in the way he had soon become tongue tied during dinner and confused his words. That was something which rarely, if ever, happened. It made him feel even worse about the relentless pressure his mother was continuing to exert on him, simply to appease those horrendous ladies with whom she associated and believed to be her friends.

Whilst Lady Charlotte didn't appear to be quite as influenced by them, she was also being subjected to the same process, only talking about her newest gowns and embroidery last night. It wasn't as if she needed to marry for money. She had plenty of her own by all accounts, to support her in an excellent standard of living throughout her life. Yet still, here she was, being thrust by the demands of Society into finding a husband quickly. Why on earth should she also be subjected to what he could only see would be a marriage of convenience between them, and therefore, denied the possibility of finding true love.

No! Despite his loyalty and love for his mother in all other respects, this was very wrong. It would be ungentlemanly of him to pretend that he was interested in her romantically when he wasn't in the least. Even if others were urging her to marry, simply for the sake of it, as far as he was concerned. Benjamin sighed inwardly, feeling as if he was at the top of a slippery slope which his mother and brother were attempting to push him down, using every opportunity they had. How on earth was he going to put a stop to it? He didn't have a clue. He also suspected now that the situation didn't stand any chance of improvement. His mother would continue pushing him into courting Lady Charlotte despite his obvious reservations.

Of course, he knew exactly what she was doing. She was waiting for him to weaken his resolve so that she could get her own way. Instead, it only created a highly unpleasant situation and a distraction he could well do without. His own life was filled with his considerable interest in the arts, friends who appreciated the same things as he did, and a love of the outdoors. He liked nothing better than to walk for hours on end at the family estate. Also, because of the effect all this was having on him, he had missed a large part of what was a very interesting lecture. Muttering to himself in frustration, he soon became determined to listen more carefully until the lecturer's words managed to successfully cut through his misery and he began to listen avidly to them.

Afterwards, feeling more refreshed, Benjamin took the opportunity to visit the circulating library and peruse the books about art on its shelves. He lost himself for a while in their pages, but decided finally to borrow a novel he had still to read, on the assumption that the story might provide the distraction he needed.

Neither Lady Rosamund nor Simon had any knowledge of Benjamin's wish to travel to see the relics of the ancient world for himself. It was outside their areas of interest, whilst to Benjamin, it truly was a treasure chest waiting to be opened. So, the last thing he wanted or needed was to have a wife at his side who didn't share his interests, which had now become a passion. Such a woman would only find him boring. Now the war with Napoleon was over and people had started to travel again, his desire for travel had only increased. Admittedly, he could leave his wife at home in England. But again this was something he wasn't prepared to countenance, wishing instead to share his life completely with her.

Nevertheless, maybe that was the answer? To absent himself from England for a while, exploring the world and his passion. That would certainly put him far beyond the clutches of Mama, and who knew what would happen when nature was allowed to take its own course? He might well fall in love and marry of his own accord. The thought made Benjamin smile once again in the way he used to as a boy, without carrying the troubles of the world on his back.

He turned his attention then to a book he had picked up by chance, concluding it must have been left on the wrong shelf. It contained a collection of works by lesser-known landscape painters, not the history he had intended to look at. The veiled woman at the Academy came to mind again, along with the feeling that she might well be a kindred spirit. He had been fascinated by her as soon as he saw the way she was staring at the landscape on the wall in front of her. It had clearly drawn her in, absorbing her imagination and senses.

When this image was quickly followed by recalling the pressure he was under to marry against his own inclinations, Benjamin couldn't help wondering if the lady also appreciated the power of art. Did she too revel in the away it was able to evoke certain emotions and take one to another time and place? It was almost as if one was travelling through history, the day in which the painter had lived, and how they had seen the world at that time. They had expressed it on canvas so that future generations could have the privilege of also being able to view it. No, he decided, however difficult the situation might currently be, he couldn't give up his passion. He wished to share his life with a woman who felt the same as he did about art. Lord Benjamin Willoughby would never marry for anything less than love!

After this revelation, Benjamin felt restless and decided to call on his favourite aunt, Lady Margaret, whose presence he had always found soothing. She was the complete opposite to her sister-in-law, his mother, and exuded an air of calm. From those far off days when he had been a young boy, he had loved spending as much time as he was allowed to with her. She had a gentle and kind disposition. It was only a short journey, so he soon arrived at her townhouse, where he was escorted by the butler into the drawing room.

Lady Margaret smiled warmly, obviously delighted to see him again despite him interrupting her reading of Miss Jane Austen's *Sense and Sensibility*. Immediately concerned by the troubled look on her nephew's face, she placed the novel on the small table next to and looked attentively at Benjamin. She said how delighted she was to see him, and then immediately asked the reason for his surprise visit.

Benjamin smiled then and told her he had simply missed her company. But she knew her nephew too well and realised that something serious was bothering him. After she had arranged for tea to be brought to them, she placed her hand gently on his arm

40

and she asked Benjamin in a soft voice why he was looking so preoccupied.

He couldn't help groaning inwardly. Maybe he shouldn't have come after all. His aunt was suffering with her health and had her own troubles to contend with.

"I'm sorry. It's just the same old story getting me down, and certainly not my intention to distress you by worrying about me," he said, trying hard to make light of how deeply events at last night's dinner were still affecting him.

Lady Margaret was not, however, prepared to give up so easily. She sat quietly with her hands clasped on her lap, patiently waiting for him to tell her everything. Although Benjamin still didn't realise it, this had been their way of going about things since he was a boy, which for some reason, his mother had never seemed to understand. Benjamin's father had seen it as clearly as his sister did, whilst Benjamin's older brother, Simon, was sadly, in Lady Margaret's opinion, the mirror image of Rosamund in so many ways. Their mother expected the world to be exactly how she wished it to be, which at times was simply ridiculous, especially in this instance.

In Lady Margaret's humble opinion, which she had so far kept to herself, it was obvious that all Rosamund was doing was making her youngest son extremely unhappy. Benjamin was more sensitive than his older brother and actually quite shy. So, Rosamund couldn't even begin to understand the effect which her insistence that Benjamin court the girl of her choice must be having on him. And her choice would not, Lady Margaret was sure, be suitable for him at all.

She was of the opinion that people were the way they were, and it wasn't for us to try to change their personalities. It should be more than enough for her sister-in-law that Benjamin was a fine, young man. It didn't make him any less of a person because he could seem a little slow and ponderous at times. It was due to him being more thoughtful and serious than Simon. That was simply his way.

Meanwhile, Benjamin began to open his heart to his aunt, as she expected him to do. He told her all about his lack of attraction or feelings for Lady Charlotte Sinclair, and how he wished for something much deeper in a marriage.

"I don't believe it's right, nor that I can pretend to do it. Especially not now Mama has become more relentless," he said earnestly, sipping the tea the housemaid had brought in.

Lady Margaret's heart went out to her nephew. Not loving him any the less now that he was a grown man, the old feeling of wishing he had been her son came rushing back to her. His life would have been very different if he had been. There certainly wouldn't have been any of this endless bullying from that dreadful woman who professed to be his mother!

Doing the only thing she could, and as she had done many times in the past, Lady Margaret tried to guide him with her words. Referring to him again as she had when he was a boy, she said, "Ben, you must follow your own heart, regardless of your mother's wishes. Marriage is a serious matter. It's very important that the bride and groom enjoy each other's company as well as there being a romantic attraction."

Benjamin didn't hear any more than that since it was enough. It was exactly what he had been thinking. It seemed his aunt's kindness and support were all that he had needed to continue with his earlier intention of staying true to himself.

After they had finished their tea, Benjamin told his aunt about his visit to the Royal Academy, and to the Minerva Press earlier that day, but for some reason, he did not mention the veiled woman who had caught his attention so strongly and about whom he had been thinking of so much. He wondered why and realised that for some inexplicable reason, he wished to keep her memory to himself.

When he was standing up and was about to take his leave, Lady Margaret asked Benjamin if he would have time to escort her the following day, as she wished to visit the shops on Bond Street. He readily agreed, delighted to be able to do something in return for the solace and love she always gave to him.

Chapter 7

A Visit To The Modiste's Shop

The following day, Sophia reluctantly agreed to accompany her friend Beatrice on a visit to the modiste who made the majority of her clothes. She had mixed feelings about the visit but didn't think it was possible to refuse on this occasion as she had done in the past. When she saw the look of dismay on her friend's face in anticipation of a refusal, she realised just how difficult it must sometimes have been for Beatrice not to give up on her. Beatrice had helped her when she had been at her most miserable and continued to do so despite Sophia's lack of progress at coming out of mourning. Even so, her friend had never complained.

Sophia told herself that she was going to have to try harder to be sociable, however miserable and depressed she still felt. None of this was Beatrice or Lady Helena's fault, and all she had done with their kindness was to make everything so much harder. I must learn to bear the grief alone, she thought resolutely. But how to do that when her thoughts were still in turmoil and her heart had yet to heal?

She also regarded a visit to the modiste as an integral part of what she thought of now as her old life, before Henry's death. One which would never return. Even though she was only twenty-three years of age, she didn't believe she would ever forget him or get beyond the fact that she was no longer a beautiful woman because of her disfigurement.

It worried her too that she didn't read the fashion magazines any longer, so she didn't even know what the modiste might make for her if Beatrice managed to persuade her to have a new gown. Irrespective of that, she thought with a twinge of guilt, she could

44

also remember how much she used to look forward to the excitement of having a new gown. Maybe even two or three at a time if she had needed them. She went through similar stages with her paintings, from planning them in detail to the thrill of seeing finished product.

She had never objected to the inconvenience of the fittings as she knew some debutantes did. She hadn't objected to any of it. Like her painting, it was a world which had once upon a time been filled with colour and light that, with Henry's dying, had turned to black.

Beatrice had attempted to persuade her on several occasions to at least begin a period of half mourning, suggesting that Sophia could gradually introduced a subdued grey, purple, and even some white into her attire. Sophia sighed to think that if only she could have made Beatrice understand how she really felt and why she simply couldn't have done it before.

Her loss, the guilt she felt at the part she had played in the tragedy, and her face being scarred had overwhelmed her. Abandoning the black simply hadn't felt appropriate. In her mind, it would have been far better if she could have turned back the clock. Obviously, she couldn't. She still berated herself for having fallen asleep on that dreadful night, at the very least, she believed she should have been able to reach Henry and wake him. She still sometimes dreamed of it and woke up with tears on her cheeks.

Her thoughts returned abruptly to the present when the carriage stopped outside the modiste's shop for she and Beatrice to alight. As soon as they had stepped down from it, Beatrice tucked Sophia's arm through her own and patted her hand before they entered the shop. They were greeted by a display of the most elegant fabrics imaginable, with Sophia being immediately drawn to their colours, imagining how she might mix the shades from her paints. The brightest were in sharp contrast to the dark, and drab mourning clothes she wore. Green had always been a particular favourite, reminding her of the new foliage as it appeared on the trees in spring. Even in the harshest of winters, which could often seem stark, there was always green of some sort. It suddenly came to her, without her understanding why, that there was a season for everything.

Beatrice had noticed almost immediately that her friend's attention seemed to be completely absorbed by the rolls of fabric. She watched as, despite being lost in thought as usual, Sophia released her arm and moved quickly from one roll of material to another, touching each one reverently. The softest of smiles played on her lips, and without being conscious of doing it, she occasionally sighed as if in in awe.

Meanwhile, Beatrice was absolutely delighted that what she had hoped might happen had come to fruition. It seemed that Sophia was at long last beginning to return from the darkest of places, where she had taken herself after Henry's death. She breathed a huge sigh of relief that she had at last guessed correctly how to help her friend. She hoped that Sophia's reaction to seeing so many beautiful fabrics was an indicator that she was willing to start a short period of half mourning before returning fully to a more colourful wardrobe. Beatrice believed it would make her friend feel so much better in herself, and that was all she wished for.

She had discussed her friend's loss with her own husband. Grateful to be very happily married to James, she had also secretly wondered how she might have coped if the tables had been turned and it had been him who died. She had cried even at the thought of it. Afterwards, she had felt she at least understood some of Sophia's thoughts, especially those times when her friend had refused to accompany her on her visits to the modiste.

James had urged his wife to carry on trying to get her friend to change her mind. Having met Sophia on a number of occasions before her marriage to Henry, he knew that being dressed in black was not her true nature. Sophia was clearly someone whose spirit shone brightly, a young woman of love and light, which had actually been Henry's own description of her when he told James that he wished to marry her. Moreover, he had declared that it would be impossible for him not to! How could he let the bright light which had come to illuminate his own dull life get away. James had been inclined to agree.

Taking Sophia's arm again as she continued to walk along the rows of bright colours, Beatrice quietly suggested that it might be time for her to consider wearing them again. Not waiting to give Sophia the opportunity to reply, she reached out to touch a beautiful green fabric which had clearly caught her friend's eye. Holding her breath, since she wasn't at all certain Sophia would comply, she asked her friend to lift up her veil.

Hesitating only for an instant before she did so, Beatrice held a small sample of the beautiful fabric against Sophia's cheek, saying she wished to see how it would look against her complexion. After a moment's thought, she encouraged Sophia to consider it for herself in the looking glass. After a moment of hesitation, she did so. Beatrice couldn't stop herself from smiling in delight, and relief, to see it. Her plan could easily have gone awry and even do more harm than good, as James had warned her, if she didn't go about it in the right way. It could have sent Sophia further into herself. But thankfully, the time for change seemed to be right after all.

Meanwhile, much to Sophia's surprise, as she looked in the mirror, she could see herself in her mind's eye wearing the most beautiful green gown made from the fabric Beatrice was still holding against her face. In the same moment as the guilt she still felt about wearing bright colours was about to rear up again within her, it was interrupted by an older woman unexpectedly greeting Beatrice as she made her way towards them.

Sophia immediately stepped away from the fabric, flustered that not only had a stranger caught her not wearing her veil, but she had also been in the act of admiring something she believed she had no right to. Before she could cover the scar on her face, her fingers trembling, Beatrice had taken her hand and whispered that she had nothing to worry about. Lady Margaret Lancaster was a close friend of her mother's, and her nature was nothing but kind.

Nevertheless, despite Beatrice's reassurances, Sophia couldn't help feeling trapped and extremely self-conscious. Especially when Beatrice did the only thing she could do and politely introduced her to Lady Margaret, who was by this time standing next to them. Much to Sophia's surprise, the woman didn't react with shock or pity at the sight of her scarred face. Instead, she offered Sophia the warmest of smiles and began to engage her straight away in pleasantries, as if nothing at all was amiss.

She instantly shared that on her last visit to the modiste she had also admired the same green fabric Sophia was looking at. Then, somewhat unbelievably to Sophia's ears, Lady Margaret remarked how beautiful it would look if was made up into a dress for her. This casual compliment made Sophia feel much more at ease, and she began to relax, while Beatrice and Lady Margaret chatted about the health of her friend's mother, who, it appeared, was prone to suffer from the most dreadful headaches.

After a while, Sophia's gaze drifted away from them to the entrance of the shop, and the street outside. She was suddenly startled to see the gentleman from the Royal Academy of Arts looking into the shop. His hand was on the door, and he appeared to be about to come inside. Not once imagining she would see him again, especially not since she was still in mourning, Sophia couldn't help but feel a flicker of warmth enter her heart. She quickly lowered her eyes before he had the opportunity of noticing her staring at him.

Chapter 8

A Surprise Meeting

After his Aunt Margaret had asked him to escort her on her shopping trip, Benjamin remembered that he had other business of his own he could attend to with his tailor, whose premises were within easy walking distance of the modiste's shop. Knowing his aunt was likely to take much longer than he did, he made his way slowly back to Bond Street to meet her, enjoying sauntering along the street in the sunshine. As soon as he was through the door of the shop, he could hear her gentle voice floating up from between the stacked bolts of fabric, where she appeared to be in earnest conversation with another lady.

He was delighted to see it, as he sometimes felt his aunt spent far too much time on her own at her townhouse, and he had no wish for her to be lonely. Benjamin approached his aunt, but he soon saw that he had made a mistake. Lady Margaret was engaged in conversation with not one but two other women. His heart skipped a beat when he realised with amazement that one of them was the young lady from the Royal Academy. She was looking across the aisle at him, and he was surprised at first that she wasn't wearing her veil. This piqued his already considerable curiosity about her, and now, her relationship with his aunt. He approached them with a smile on his face, intending to share in their obvious delight in each other's company.

His Aunt Margaret returned his smile as soon as she saw him and wasted no time in taking his arm and introducing him to Lady Beatrice Stanhope and Lady Sophia Montgomery. Both young ladies curtsied politely, while he bowed and expressed his pleasure at being introduced to them both. However, his eyes lingered on Lady Sophia, certain she would remember him from the Academy. However, disappointingly, she avoided meeting his eyes at all. Not knowing the reason for it, especially when she had been looking directly at him as he was walking towards them, he attributed her withdrawal to either extreme shyness or embarrassment. He couldn't help noticing that the scarring on the right side of her face seemed quite prominent that morning, flaring an angry red, which he imagined must have been of considerable concern to her.

Benjamin's heart reached out to hers. He wished in that moment that he could voice his feelings and reassure her that, in his own eyes, she was a very beautiful woman. She was someone he would like to get to know a lot better! He had taken the view for a long time that none of us were perfect, whether in physical appearance or otherwise. Although he understood perfectly well that her scar would cause others to stare, it didn't bother him in the least. He only wished to know the reason for it and be certain that she would still hold her head up high.

His thoughts returned to the way she had been entranced by the landscape at the Academy. He knew intuitively from that how deeply she must feel what her eyes saw, and no doubt, what her ears heard. A momentary sadness passed through him when he thought of how difficult her life must be to have such a disfigurement at a time when Society held its own view of perfection in such high regard.

Benjamin tried hard not to stare at her face, although his eyes continued to betray him. Again, he wasn't looking at the scar, but he longed for her eyes to meet his so that he could look deeply into them. He also felt an overwhelming need to speak to her and know all of her story. Much to his frustration, good manners dictated that he had to wait quietly and politely next to his aunt while she continued her conversation with two young ladies. Mostly, they talked about the different fabrics and styles they fancied for their new gowns. This somewhat surprised him since his Aunt Margaret at least had never appeared much interested in fashion, and Lady Sophia was dressed all in black, clearly mourning someone.

Strangely, he found the conversation didn't irritate him in the way it usually did when his mother spoke about such things. He actually found it quite charming, listening to them talk quietly as they considered the merits of each fabric. It was even more to his delight when Lady Sophia waxed quite animatedly about the green material she was holding up to the light, and it touched his heart again. Before that moment, she had mostly been standing quietly next to Lady Beatrice, listening to her talking to his aunt, adding very little to the conversation. She had only contributed when asked a direct question.

He considered her appearance, which could only be described as exceedingly drab. Black didn't suit her, in his opinion. He was glad for her if she found some pleasure in admiring the glorious green fabric she seemed to favour. He wasn't surprised in the least about her interest in colour, though, having convinced himself by then that she must be a painter. He was thrilled to spot what he saw as proof of this speculation in a small patch of green oil paint which she had either not been able to remove from her dress or had failed to notice.

After only a few minutes, which for Benjamin passed far too soon, the modiste's assistant called Lady Beatrice and Lady Sophia away. As a result, they were all obliged to part, much to Benjamin's regret, leaving him with the distinct impression that Lady Sophia was glad to be able to make her escape.

Once his aunt had attended to her own affairs with the modiste, she and Benjamin agreed it would be very pleasant to visit Gunter's tea shop. The thought of its delicious, cooling ices on such a warm day was highly appealing to him. After they had placed their order and taken their seats among the other ladies and gentlemen with had the same idea, Benjamin decided it was a good time to quiz his aunt about Lady Sophia Montgomery. Since he wasn't certain he should reveal too much of an interest in her, he said, tentatively at first, "I hope you have enjoyed your morning's shopping, Aunt Margaret, and found conversing with, if may I say, two such delightful ladies agreeable."

He hesitated when Lady Margaret looked pointedly at him, clearly trying to read between the lines.

Benjamin pressed on regardless. "Um, I was wondering how you know Lady Sophia and Lady Beatrice."

Lady Margaret paused while Benjamin took another mouthful of his ice before she replied.

"It was the first time I have met Lady Sophia, actually, although I know Beatrice and her mother quite well. They informed me of Lady Sophia's tragic story."

"Story? What story?" he asked, all ears. He listened with rapt attention as Lady Margaret repeated what she knew of the fire and how Lady Sophia's face was disfigured. She elaborated, telling him that Lady Sophia was only now starting to be seen again in Society. When digesting all the tragic details, Benjamin felt his stomach churning. He couldn't begin to imagine Lady Sophia's suffering, and all because of a fire shortly after her marriage, resulting in the loss of her husband. And worse, it appeared they had been very much in love. Somehow, he couldn't imagine her marrying for anything less that love.

He listened with concern to the extent of the hardships which his aunt, and possibly Lady Clara Stanhope, had surmised Sophia had endured. Quite unexpectedly then, because it was the first he had heard of it, and it was unusual for his aunt to do any such thing, she revealed she was planning to host a soiree and was considering extending an invitation to Lady Sophia. It would only be a small affair, she hastened to add, because she knew that Lady Sophia was about to enter a short period of half mourning and hadn't yet returned fully to Society. She failed to mention that she and Lady Clara, Beatrice's mother, were counting on Beatrice to persuade Lady Sophia to attend.

Although Benjamin was careful not to show any further interest in Lady Sophia at that point, his spirits soared. He immediately told his aunt that he thought it was a wonderful idea for her to arrange a soiree. Secretly, he prayed that Lady Sophia would accept his aunt's invitation. The truth of the matter was, he couldn't wait to see her again.

Chapter 9

The Gentleman with the Kind Eyes

Meanwhile, as the modiste took her measurements for a new gown, Sophia was filled with thoughts of Lord Benjamin Willoughby. She had been persuaded by Beatrice to take her friend's fitting appointment, and Sophia had been encouraged to agree after seeing all of the beautiful fabrics on display. Also, though it was known only to herself, she had been prompted by the arrival of Lord Willoughby, whom she certainly hadn't expected to see again. Especially not while visiting the modiste's shop.

As the modiste's assistant skilfully took her measurements and made a note of them, Sophia couldn't stop thinking about Lord Willoughby. Nor did she really want to,. His intense gaze had made her feel self-conscious at first, but his demeanour was so quiet and gentle, she had eventually begun to relax. He was much like his Aunt Margaret, with whom she had soon felt at ease. Except for the delicious butterflies in her stomach which she also felt when he was nearby.

It had come to her with a start then, that Lord Benjamin Willoughby had the kindest eyes she had ever seen. Apart from Henry's, of course, she thought guiltily, almost as soon as the thought entered her head. Nevertheless, she couldn't help feeling dismayed when she began to wonder if he pitied her or found her appearance repulsive because of the scar. He had seen her twice now without her veil.

Her thoughts were interrupted by Beatrice, who had been talking to her quietly in the background about the fitting of her own dress. Still in a state of considerable excitement, she told Sophia that she couldn't wait to see how she would look in her new green dress. This was an ordinary remark, something which Sophia realised they might well said to each other when they used to go shopping before her marriage to Henry. She realised Beatrice was trying hard to make her feel comfortable about her circumstances. Feeling a great wave of affection, she made herself smile at her friend. In seeing Beatrice's happy expression, it struck Sophia how much she had enjoyed the experience of having a new dress made, along with the anticipation of wearing it. It seemed her life was starting to move forward again, without any real intervention from her. She pondered if it was as both Beatrice and Lady Helena had been saying all along; that it would happen when the time was right.

Sophia and Beatrice spent the next hour looking in several other shops, travelling by hackney carriage when the distance between the shops they wished to visit was too far for them to walk. Sophia also noticed the Gallery of the British Institution in Pall Mall when they went past it. She would have liked to see the exhibition being shown there, but knowing the paintings wouldn't be to her friend's taste, she didn't mention it. Henry would, she knew, have liked it as much as her, which reminded her of him again and of something else which she now missed doing with him.

Unknown to Beatrice, the worrying conversation Sophia had had with Henry's lawyer was niggling constantly at the back of her mind. As they continued shopping, she recalled Mr Blackwood's warning about her dire financial position and began to wonder if she shouldn't start being more frugal. She sighed to herself then, for, as Lady Helena had pointed out, the matter needed to be looked into.

But in the end, she decided she needn't spoil the day by worrying about the solicitor's words that morning. Even if the worst happened, it surely won't be for some time, she reassured herself. So, she tried to regain the excitement she had felt earlier at the modiste's shop and suggested to Beatrice that they should possibly pay a particular nearby haberdashery a visit.

Both of them were stunned by the array of beautiful trimmings and colours which met their eyes when they stepped into the shop. It wasn't long before Sophia wished to buy some pretty ribbon, which she was certain would be useful for any number of things. This was all much to Beatrice's delight, and she made no secret of the fact that she was overjoyed to see her friend taking an interest in clothes again. So much so that a conversation followed as to whether Sophia would allow her to purchase the ribbon for her as a gift, which she finally agreed to after some vigorous persuasion.

By this time, Beatrice confessed she was feeling tired, so they decided to return to Sophia's townhouse for tea. When they were comfortably seated in the drawing room, to take advantage of the sunlight coming in through the windows, the maid brought their tea along with a plate of biscuits. Beatrice's eyes were full of sympathy when she asked Sophia if she was considering re-entering Society.

"The mere thought of it makes my stomach churn," Sophia admitted. In fact, it made her feel so uncomfortable that she put down the biscuit she had been eating. "I think I need a little more time to adjust. I have been considering it, though." She didn't want to say she feared having insufficient confidence in her appearance, or that she was unsure if she could really cope with any unpleasantness which might be directed at her because of the scar. |Thankfully, Beatrice didn't pursue the matter any further but carried on drinking her tea, for which Sophia was grateful. If she was honest, going back into Society still seemed an enormously daunting challenge she was not sure she wanted to face.

After the two ladies had kissed each other affectionately on the cheek and Beatrice had taken her leave, Sophia was soon joined in the drawing room by Lady Helena. It took her several minutes before she revealed the reason for her visit, other than it being solely a social call. Sophia was stunned to learn that she had received an unexpected letter from Vincent, Henry's estranged brother. Her mother-in-law said that she had been equally shocked herself when the letter was brought into the drawing room for her to open. So far as both of them knew, Henry hadn't seen or heard from Vincent for a long time, and neither had they.

Helena handed the letter to Sophia so that she could read its contents for herself and, as her mother-in-law said, gain a better impression of the reason for it being sent. However, the letter didn't furnish either of them with any further understanding of this. Once Sophia had finished reading it, she looked at Lady Helena questioningly. The letter was short and to the point. It simply stated that Vincent intended to visit them soon, referring to both of them as the remnants of his dear family.

Sophia continued looking at Lady Helena for support and guidance in the matter. When her mother-in-law didn't say anything else but still appeared to be shocked, she asked her if she thought Vincent might be returning to claim his title.

Helena frowned then and admitted she hoped it was his intention, as it would be the right and proper thing to do. This was, of course, irrespective of the fallout between Henry's father and Vincent all those years ago, which his younger brother had inevitably been drawn into. Unfortunately, as Lady Helena explained, Henry had been forced to take sides and had inevitably chosen to follow his dear papa's guidance and advice.

Sophia was, however, left with mixed feelings regarding the unexpected news of her brother-in-law's impending visit, especially when a firm date had not been suggested. She had known the family for many years including Vincent, and she had liked him. He was, after all, her late husband's brother, so he had shared many similarities to Henry. But things had changed once the boys had grown older.

From the little that Henry had told her about it, Vincent had never really settled at anything which would make him a living. He had expected instead to inherit his father's fortune as the eldest son, without having to work for it or indeed put in much effort. He chose to ignore the fact that their father had worked hard to increase the small fortune he had inherited and regarded it as his own eldest son's duty to do the same.

The final straw in the fall out between the two brothers came after their father's death. Vincent had inherited a large sum from their father, which ran through his fingers like water. This resulted in him unjustly accusing Henry of being spiteful when he refused to help him repay his creditors. Sophia wasn't certain that Lady Helena was aware of that aspect of it, so she didn't say anything. But at the same time, she hoped Vincent wasn't simply coming back for financial reasons.

Sophia also wondered why it had to happen now, when she had just rediscovered the joy of painting, had a lovely morning at the modiste's shop, and talked to both Beatrice and Lady Margaret. She had started to believe she would like to return to Society, albeit the quieter parts of it. Also, almost without even daring to admit it to herself, she had experienced the thrill of meeting the unknown yet appealing gentleman from the Royal Academy.

She thought now that her memory hadn't served her well, as he was, in truth, considerably more handsome than she had recalled. Lord Benjamin Willoughby had the kindest of eyes, which made her feel drawn to him. I certainly hope Vincent's visit won't spoil any of that for me, she thought, all the while fearing that it might well do so. For there was something else she recalled about Vincent from their childhood; he often left a trail of misery and destruction wherever he went, much to the dismay of all who knew him.

Sophia looked at Lady Helena, who was staring down at the letter with what appeared to be determination, presumably to

59

remain loyal to her eldest son. Despite what might have occurred in the past, now he had decided to offer them his affection and support. Sophia knew only too well how much change the future could bring, and that it wasn't always for the better. She feared privately that Vincent's letter might not be the good news Lady Helena was hoping it was.

At the same time, she felt guilty at being more concerned about how Vincent's arrival would affect her progress in recovering from the loss of Henry. There was also a valid concern that as her eldest male relative, Vincent might well try to control her affairs. Even though she didn't trust him, he could, for instance, easily object to her no longer being in mourning for his brother. If she had even succeeded in coming out of it by the time he arrived, that was.

Sophia admitted to herself that most of all she couldn't help yearning to see Lord Benjamin Willoughby again, and she was afraid now that Vincent would refuse to give his approval to her doing so.

Chapter 10

An Unexpected Visitor

The following morning, Lady Helena joined Sophia for breakfast in her drawing room. They had decided to meet earlier than usual to offer each other support because of the ways in which the news of Vincent's unexpected return had, for different reasons, quite overwhelmed them. They both knew it was something which would, without the shadow of a doubt, have an effect on their lives.

Lady Helena had persuaded herself that her eldest son's return could well be a blessing in disguise. His father had fallen out with him years ago, as a result of a matter in which she had not felt able to interfere. She had been forced to trust her late husband's judgement. At the time, she had privately taken the view that the fallout was due solely to petty jealousy. Her two sons, she claimed, had both been guilty of it as children, and it appeared to have continued into their adult lives.

Not that Henry was ever aware of what had actually transpired, she told Sophia, since his father had thought it better that his youngest son didn't know the truth. Although Lady Helena had objected to Vincent being disinherited when he had complained to her that Papa had threatened him with it should he continue to defy his wishes.

She confessed to Sophia that she was feeling more than a little affected by the onset of age and her ongoing responsibilities, especially following the death of Henry, whom she had become used to relying on. So much so, that she could now easily believe she would welcome Vincent's support. His return to the fold represented the perfect opportunity to pass being the head of the family onto him, something which was his by right anyway, after his father and brother's deaths. She also took the view that Vincent would be able to solve the problem which Sophia was experiencing with Mr Blackwood much better than she ever could, for it had been worrying her since she had learned of it.

She admitted her eldest son did have a dark side, and his secretive nature was unfortunately part of that. She frowned when she remembered some of the things he had done as a boy.

"But I'm sure he must have changed for the better. He's a grown man now, after all," she said in a tone that Sophia thought sounded like she wanted to convince herself of it.

Sophia still wasn't quite as certain that she wished for her brother-in-law's return. Hadn't they been managing admirably until now? Without Vincent's interference. She had trusted her late husband's opinion of his brother when Vincent asked him for the funds to repay his creditors, and she had never had any reason to doubt it. Henry had taken the view that the money from his own trust fund would be unlikely to be repaid because of his brother's rakish lifestyle and generally lackadaisical manner. Vincent had soon lost his temper with that attitude, which she recalled he had been prone to do when they were children, accusing Henry of not being a gentleman, which she knew was far removed from the truth.

However, she saw no point in repeating any of this to Lady Helena, though she risked risking the possibility of creating a rift between herself and Lady Helena, who, if she ever found out, might consider that her daughter-in-law hadn't been entirely truthful with her. Besides, Sophia reasoned, it was all in the past. Far better to give her brother-in-law the benefit of the doubt until she met him again. After all, people did sometimes change, and his own life may be back on track again. The problem would be, of course, if he hadn't changed, then his return could be detrimental to both herself and her beloved mother-in-law.

Now, Sophia also felt unable to tell Lady Helena about the progress she had recently made in coming out of herself and that she had seriously started to think about no longer being in mourning. Despite a part of her still feeling that it would be a betrayal of Henry's memory, she believed that she wouldn't be able to bear it if Lady Helena took the view that it was still too early. Despite what Sophia had taken earlier as encouragement from her mother-in-law that she should return to Society, it no longer seemed the right time to raise the issue. Especially not since her mother-in-law continued to dress in dark clothing herself.

In truth, meeting Lord Benjamin Willoughby had confused and delighted Sophia in equal measure. Irrespective of everything else, she couldn't help but feel now that she wished not only to retain his acquaintance but allow it to develop naturally. Although she hadn't yet admitted to herself that this might possibly also include a romance. However, it turned out, though, she again didn't feel able to make an announcement to Lady Helena that she had quite by chance met a gentleman she really liked, especially whilst Lady Helena had so many other things on her mind. Sophia loved her too dearly to burden her any further with her own thoughts and problems. Apart from, of course, the issue she had with Mr Blackwood, from which she feared she might not be able to recover if what he feared came to pass and she really was destitute.

She also wasn't certain that her growing attraction to Lord Benjamin Willoughby and the possibility of being left penniless were appropriate topics of conversation to discuss with Beatrice. Despite them being close, Beatrice and her husband had liked Henry a lot, so they could see it as a betrayal of sorts.

Regarding her finances, the truth of the matter was she would find it exceedingly difficult to bear the shame of destitution. Sophia's face paled, as she looked down at her breakfast plate, and the thought came to her then that she must think of herself as being fortunate now. She might not always have enough to eat, or a soft bed to sleep in, with her own roof over her head. Tears trickled slowly down her cheeks, while as Lady Helena put another dainty morsel of bacon in her mouth, completely lost in her own affairs, completely failing to notice how upset her daughter-in-law had become. It seemed that silent support is all we can offer each other, Sophia thought as she quietly wiped her face in a most unladylike manner with her napkin so it wouldn't seem as if she had been crying.

Lady Helena glanced at Sophia then and noticed how pale she looked. She was no doubt worrying again about her youngest son's lawyer. However, since it was unlikely to be too much longer before Vincent arrived, she decided that she could, after all, leave the matter entirely to him to deal with, including deciding how large a provision she would need to make for Sophia's welfare if need be.

She hesitated then before beginning to talk about him, since she didn't know exactly how much Sophia knew of what had happened in the past. Deciding not to give away too much about this, but to say something fairly general she made the suggestion that Vincent was likely to have seen the error of his ways, and she felt certain that he would be intending to honour Henry's title which had passed to him under his late brother's will.

She added that it would be highly beneficial to have a relative who could look into both of their finances. She had included her own affairs to show Sophia that she supported Vincent's judgement in such matters, even though she remained quite happy with how her late husband had organised her own before his death. Her situation was very comfortable indeed and would be for the rest of her life. However, she ought to have added the caveat to this that it was, provided nothing changed.

Although Sophia couldn't help feeling sceptical about Vincent having become a better man now, she couldn't deny that

64

he was Lady Helena's eldest son, and she owed it to her mother-in-law to at least consider the possibility that his help would be beneficial. But then Soames appeared with a silver salver in his hand, and Sophia took the sealed letter from the tray. This was an occurrence which would usually have caused some excitement amongst the two ladies, but not on this occasion, both were a little too preoccupied for that. Nevertheless, Sophia's eyes widened in shock when she opened it and discovered it was an invitation to attend Lady Margaret Lancaster's soiree, in three days' time.

Without being able to stop it from happening, Sophia's earlier anxiety she felt about her appearance resurfaced. Surely, she couldn't attend the soiree wearing her veil or in a mourning dress, could she? Lady Helena, once she had seen the invitation, told her gently that it would be a good idea for her to accept and use the engagement as a way to re-enter Society. Henry wouldn't have wanted or expected her to hide herself away forever. When she insisted Sophia must begin now to think about it like that, Sophia only nodded, since Lady Helena wasn't aware of her interest in Lord Benjamin Willoughby.

After their breakfast was finished and her mother-in-law had left to get on with her own arrangements for the day, Sophia decided to go for a walk in Hyde Park. She was hoping to be able to clear her confused state of mind, for she felt she already had quite enough to think about before worrying about the questions Vincent's immanent arrival posed. Realising she was about to become overwhelmed again, she decided on the spur of the moment to take her sketchbook with her, just in case she found the opportunity to add some further drawings while she was out.

Sophia went upstairs to put on her bonnet, deciding that it wasn't the time to show herself off in fashionable clothes, as would have been the case if she had been wearing a new gown in an open carriage. Although she had from time to time enjoyed doing that with Henry. It would be wonderful now to simply be outside in the fresh air and enjoy the exercise.

She hoped that wearing her black mourning dress would help to make her appear invisible to those who were out and about in the park. She knew she must reply to Lady Margaret's invitation without much delay, so she resolved to make a final decision whether to attend while she was out. Sophia sighed, feeling the beginnings of a headache, and she reminded herself how much she loved to see the trees and flowers at the park, and also the horses. The gentlemen often rode through the park at this time of day, at Rotten Row. It was a popular spot, where ladies and gentlemen expected to be seen and admired by others, but she and Lizzie could easily avoid it.

Once they arrived at Hyde Park, it wasn't long before they found a reasonably secluded bench not far inside the entrance. Sophia began to sketch an early flowering rose bush which was partially in bloom. It was one of the most beautiful she had ever seen, although its name escaped her. Lizzie sat quietly gazing around in wonder at her surroundings, and occasionally at the sketch book, to admire her ladyship's skill with a pencil.

Chapter 11

Sophia Sketches a Rose

Meanwhile, Lord Benjamin Willoughby was sitting in his study, staring miserably at the opposite wall when his butler knocked at the door to deliver a letter laid on a small silver salver. Seeing his mother's elegant handwriting on the envelope, Benjamin reluctantly picked it up, and his stomach started churning once again. He was even more dismayed to discover that it was in fact a reminder from Lady Rosamund, concerning his agreement to escort her to the dinner that evening, which was being hosted by Charlotte's mother, Lady Lucy Sinclair. He had tried his best to forget all about it, for he had been secretly dreading the evening since the moment he first learned of it.

Benjamin groaned, deciding that he might as well regard his entire day as ruined before it had even begun. Then, he spoke quite sternly to himself about that being a ridiculous way to behave. He told himself that he should instead focus on going riding in Hyde Park. A ride would clear his head, for he always found riding exhilarating. After that, he was meeting his friend Robert for a round of fencing. He almost convinced himself how fortunate he was to be able to spend his time in such enjoyable ways, resolving to make the best of the day. In the meantime, there was nothing he could do about his mother's interference, and the evening was still hours away.

As he rode through the park, enjoying the breeze which ruffled his hair, he did feel better for a while. But eventually, he found his thoughts racing once again. The situation really was impossible! However hard he tried, he couldn't stop himself from thinking about the deplorable dinner he was expected to endure later, and his mother's expectations of how he ought to behave during it. Probably Lady Charlotte's too, and her mother was now about to join in!

Benjamin imagined then that the whole affair had been arranged for their benefit, simply to secure a marriage proposal from him. It really was too bad, and he knew it was inevitable that his mother would, throughout the entire evening, continue to push him towards the woman *she* had chosen to be his wife—though his heart would be constantly telling him otherwise.

Thankfully, Aunt Margaret agreed with his point of view, or he really would be feeling entirely alone. The smile returned to his lips when he thought of her gentleness, and, thankfully, how different she was to his own mother. Sad as it was to think such a thing, it really wasn't any wonder that he much preferred to be in her company rather than his own mother's. If only Lady Rosamund could see that all she was doing by interfering was pushing him away, and by doing do, she had almost spoiled their relationship beyond repair.

These thoughts were going through his mind as his horse cantered around a bend in the path, when Benjamin noticed with surprise that a woman dressed in black was sitting quietly on a bench a shirt distance away. She was holding a sketchbook in one hand and a pencil in the other. A closer look at her confirmed what his heart had secretly been hoping—it was Lady Sophia Montgomery!

The sight of her, with her veil lifted from her face, caught him off guard, and he couldn't help but be drawn to her. Observing her from a distance, he was completely captivated by the way she appeared to be fully absorbed in her work. It was just as she had appeared when she had been studying the landscape at the Royal Academy. It was impossible not to be intrigued by her, and her obvious interest art.

All thoughts of his mother and the evening ahead forgotten, Benjamin took a deep breath and slowed his horse to a trot, pulling up the reins to stop near where Lady Sophia was sitting with her maid, so that he could dismount and approach them. However, his sudden presence startled them both. Lady Sophia dropped her sketchbook onto the ground, and in that moment, she and

Benjamin stared at each other for what would most certainly have been deemed a scandalously long time by any one of the ladies of the ton.

However, what he might have regarded as a tender moment was soon interrupted by Sophia averting her eyes from his, her cheeks pink. She bent down to pick up her sketchbook, but Benjamin was too quick and reached for it first. He allowed his gaze to fall on the unfinished sketch of the rose, a simple enough subject, but the skill of execution completely took his breath away. It was exquisite, one of the most beautiful things he had ever seen. Apart from the depth of feeling he had just seen in her eyes when she looked at him.

Chapter 12

A Dress for Lady Margaret's Soiree

Sophia felt her heart miss a beat while she watched the very handsome Lord Benjamin Willoughby study her unfinished sketch, with what she knew from Beatrice was an expert eye. Given that he was a patron of the arts at the Royal Academy. She could feel herself cringing until she could see that he appeared to be genuinely impressed by her work, which caused her cheeks to flush in embarrassment. Even more so when he handed the sketchbook back to her, and their fingers accidentally brushed against each other. The touch sent a delicious shiver down the full length of her spine, and she was grateful that he could not see how he affected her.

"Thank you," she murmured shyly, clutching the sketchbook tightly in her hands, feeling a pressing need to escape the intensity of the moment. She had no idea how to deal with the regard she now had for Lord Willoughby, which appeared to be growing with each meeting. It was especially hard when he looked at her like that, with his smile reaching his eyes, allowing her to see the gentleness of spirit within them which caused her heart to melt.

She was stunned when he complimented her sketch, saying she had accurately and skilfully captured the beauty of the rose. His kind and gentle words, along with his clear appreciation of her sketch, soon soothed Sophia's nerves, and she began to relax.

At that point, Lizzie decided to go for a stroll, keeping at a discrete distance. Left with a modicum of privacy, Sophia and Lord Willoughby immediately launched into a passionate conversation about their mutual interest in painting and artists.

Sophia noticed once again that Lord Willoughby didn't stare at her scar but acted as if it wasn't there, in the way that others had used to speak to her before the fire. As they continued to converse about their own artistic preferences and the styles of their favourite artists, Sophia found herself thoroughly enjoying the exchange. It was just a refreshingly normal conversation, where she told him that she liked John Constable's landscapes, whilst he agreed they were admirable but added that he leaned more towards William Turner. Both of them were, however, in mutual agreement that Nature's beauty and her many moods were at the heart of all successful artistic endeavour.

This caused them to stare at each other again in surprise, both of them finding it difficult to believe that they should think along the same lines, then clearly enjoying the moment as it drew them closer to each other. Sophia felt more at ease than she had done in a long time. She quite forgot her earlier concerns that no one would ever speak to her again without being preoccupied with staring at her disfigurement, and that even conversing with another gentleman would somehow be letting Henry down.

She was delighted when Lord Willoughby mentioned his aunt's soiree.

"Will you be in attendance, Lady Sophia?" he asked, his eyes bright with expectation. "I know my aunt is hoping very much that you will."

Her heart skipping, Sophia made an instant decision.

"I am honoured to be invited, and I am looking forward to it very much," she told him truthfully, smiling at the prospect of them seeing each other again so soon.

"I too," he said, his lovely, kind eyes twinkling in a way that made her feel suddenly weak. "I hope we can continue our fascinating conversation about art. It is not often I have the pleasure of meeting someone who shares my passion," he added.

71

"Oh, you are so right, Lord Willoughby," Sophia agreed, nodding. "It makes such a pleasant change to talk to someone with the same interests, for it is quite rare in Society, as you point out."

They continued to talk and laugh for a while longer, and Sophia sensed it when she and Lord Willoughby both seemed to realise they had probably been speaking for a little longer than propriety dictated. There was, she noted, a definite air of reluctance as they prepared to say their goodbyes. If Nature was allowed to follow her true course, she thought with some frustration, we would just carry on talking as long as we liked.

But sadly, the time came when Lord Willoughby remounted his horse and, with a tip of his hat and a cheery smile, was soon gone from sight. Sophia watched with sinking heart, already missing his company.

Lizzie quickly returned to the bench, her face full of smiles.

"I hope you don't mind me saying so, my lady, but Lord Willoughby is a very handsome gentleman," she said, taking the sketchbook from under Sophia's arm so that she could carry it back to the carriage for her. Sophia was unable to respond, for her heart was pounding too loudly, and she knew her cheeks were flushed. It was almost as if Lizzie had read her thoughts, and while it was embarrassing to be caught out, it was also somehow comforting to know her maid agreed that His Lordship was indeed exceedingly handsome.

Not wishing to dismiss thoughts of Lord Willoughby from her mind and desperately wishing to see him again as soon as possible, once Sophia was home again, she immediately accepted Lady Margaret's invitation. Feeling happier than she had in a long time, she spent the rest of the day with her paintbox and canvas, happily immersed in her painting.

At the same time, while she worked, she derived much pleasure from replaying her unexpected meeting with Lord

Willoughby and their interesting conversation in her mind. She marvelled at his ability to make her feel so much better about herself just by the way he looked at her, In fact, he made her feel so much better about everything!

Later, Sophia changed her dress and joined Lady Helena for dinner.

"I have decided to accept Lady Margaret's invitation to her soiree," she told the older woman over the soup.

"That's wonderful news, dear," said her mother-in-law, smiling at her approvingly. "What shall you wear?"

Good question, Sophia thought, deciding this was the optimum moment to mention her change of heart over coming out of black.

"Um, I thought I might wear something a little lighter than usual," she ventured, watching Lady Helena's face carefully. "Purple, perhaps, or grey."

To her surprise, Lady Helena smiled again and nodded. "That is good news, dear. Half mourning is perfectly fitting now, I believe, and such an event is ideal for your re-entry to Society," she said, then added as if in afterthought, "Lilac would suit you."

Sophia was both relieved and thrilled to have her mother-in-law's approval.

"Oh, I had not thought of lilac," she said, frowning. "I don't have anything in that shade. Only the dark purple, and I'm afraid that has paint on it. And it's too late to have anything made up in time."

"Not to worry, dear, I have a lovely gown in lilac, with a black lace trim. Give it to Lizzie. I'm sure she can alter it in time to fit you perfectly." Lady Helena said, sipping her coffee.

"Oh, thank you! That is very generous of you. I'll ask Lizzie as soon as breakfast is over," Sophia replied, feeling optimistic that Lizzie would be able to work miracles with her needle. So, after breakfast, the two women went to Lady Helena's chambers and collected the dress. Then, once in her own chambers, Sophia rang for Lizzie. When she appeared and saw the gown, the maid became excited.

"It's lovely," she said, fingering the lilac satin admiringly. "And it will look beautiful on you, my lady, with just a few little adjustments. I'm so happy to see you going out at last and wearing something a little brighter than that awful black."

"I know, but it just has not felt quite right to go into half mourning until now," Sophia told her, wondering if her maid was recalling the lively meeting with Lord Willoughby in the park and was reading her mistress's private thoughts again. But the girl seemed truly happy for her.

They spent the next hour or so with Sophia standing in the dress on a chair, while Lizzie, her mouth full of pins, expertly pinned the side seams and turned up the hem, which was a little too long.

"It will look a treat on you, my lady," Lizzie assured Sophia once all the pins were in place. "And it won't take me long to make the alterations. It will be pressed and ready for you for the soiree."

"Thank you, Lizzie. You are a marvel. I am very grateful," Sophia told her, pleased her plans were going so well. In truth, she could not wait to see herself in the altered dress, and any traces of guilt she felt at being disloyal to Henry faded into the background. If Lady Helena, Beatrice, and Lizzie all approved of the change in costume, Sophia felt she could not be doing anything that cold be seen as disrespectful towards her former husband. What they would say if they knew she was thinking more and more of a certain gentleman, she did not know, and resolved to cross that bridge once she came to it.

Chapter 13

Falling in Love

After forcing himself to bid Lady Sophia goodbye, Benjamin reluctantly left the park and rode over to Robert's house for a round of fencing. He was looking forward to seeing his old friend again and brushing up on his fencing skills. Both of them had learned the art of fencing at Angelo's Fencing Academy in Old Bond Street and still enjoyed practising their swordsmanship with each other.

Robert greeted him cheerfully, and they were soon donning their masks and wielding their epées, assuming the correct position to challenge each other. However, the more they fenced, the more difficult Benjamin found it to concentrate on his movements.

"What on earth is wrong with you, old man?" Robert inquired after Benjamin bungled a move for the third time. "There's something on your mind. I can tell. You might as well tell me, or we'll never get anywhere."

Benjamin hesitated to answer. He wasn't certain that he wished to reveal his growing feelings for Lady Sophia to his friend. Robert might become alarmed by such erratic behaviour on his part, as it was completely out of character for him. Even to the point, he suspected, of making him seem a little odd.

"Don't tell me," Robert said drily when Benjamin didn't reply at once. He lifted his mask and, when Benjamin followed suit, stared at him searchingly. "It's a woman, isn't it?"

"How-how can you tell?" Benjamin asked, flabbergasted at his friend's intuition and feeling put on the spot.

"Well, let me put it this way, I've never seen such a silly look on your face in all the time I've known you. It's not like you. That means it must be something . . . unusual troubling you. Therefore, I conclude, it must be a certain lady who is making you act like a milksop." Robert smiled at him indulgently.

"I say, that's a bit strong," Benjamin protested.

"Not at all. I could be a lot more insulting if you prefer."

"No, no, that's quite all right," Benjamin assured him hastily.

"So, are you in love then?" Robert enquired.

Benjamin snorted. "Love! I should say . . ." He trailed off, visions of Lady Sophia's smile popping into his head and making his heart turn over in his chest.

"I see I've touched a sensitive spot," Robert said with a teasing smile. "Who is she? Is it that young lady your mother likes so much? What's her name?"

"Lady Charlotte," Benjamin filled in dully, the thought of the evening ahead and having to dine with the lady and her parents filling him with fresh dread. He frowned with irritation at the way it displaced the pleasant visions of Lady Sophia from his thoughts. "No. It's not her. Unfortunately."

Robert's brows flew up. "Oh? Who, then?"

"I don't want to say just now," he admitted, unwilling to talk about Lady Sophia with anyone else, not even his best friend. For the time being, he decided, she's all mine. "Perhaps I'll be able to say more if I get through this wretched dinner tonight in one piece," he told Robert in an appeasing tone.

Robert nodded. "Very well, my friend. I look forward to hearing about her." He pulled down his mask and assumed the position. "Now, en guarde!"

Remaining in a confused state of mind throughout the day, Benjamin added to it the sense of unease he began to feel when he called at his mother's townhouse in the early evening. He intended to keep his word and escort her to the dinner being hosted by Lady Charlotte's mother, however reluctant he was. To make matters worse, in the carriage on the way, his mother reminded him again of her expectations that he should marry well, impressing upon him afresh that it was his duty to do so.

This annoyed Benjamin greatly, for her words intruded on a wonderful image he had been harbouring of Lady Sophia on his arm as he showed her the full extent of the treasures at the Royal Academy and various galleries across London. Unfortunately, that pleasant vison soon became entangled with an opposing one of Lady Charlotte Sinclair clutching his arm tightly, while his mother walked behind them demanding that she shouldn't release him. By the time the carriage reached its destination, Benjamin felt thoroughly disheartened about what lay ahead. His mother took the opportunity to tell him to stop looking so miserable and put a smile on his face.

Not wishing to argue any further with her, accepting that to do so would be pointless, Benjamin tried to rearrange his features into a look which he thought she might find more acceptable. Looking pleased, she seized on this as proof of his intention to court Lady Charlotte that evening, much to Benjamin's increasing frustration.

After they arrived at the Sinclair residence and were escorted by the butler into the drawing room, Benjamin and his mother were warmly welcomed by Lady Lucy, while Charlotte stood quietly next to her. Politeness dictated that Benjamin should engage in mundane conversation with the pair. There were a few other guests present, but he had the distinct feeling, judging by the attentions the Ladies Lucy and Charlotte lavished on him, that he was somehow considered the star attraction.

He finally managed to escape to speak to a gentleman who was a member of one of his clubs, which was a great but temporary relief. From the corner of his eye, he could see his mother making a tactical assessment of the room. She clearly wasn't prepared to lose the advantage of their proximity to Lady Charlotte and her mother, or allow any of the other mamas who were present to steal it from her. He listened as she claimed to feel dizzy and insisted that the three of them sat down immediately for a few minutes, to wait for it to pass.

Lady Lucy readily agreed to this suggestion and ordered a glass of water to be brought for her guest. Wary but concerned for his mother's welfare, Benjamin returned to her side, and found himself one more caught up in the company of Lady Lucy and her daughter. It was a relief when the butler formally announced that dinner was ready to be served.

Unfortunately, it made little difference to him, for he was inevitably seated next to Lady Charlotte, who prattled away to him throughout the meal. But Benjamin barely heard a word she said, merely nodding and smiling periodically. His thoughts continued to dwell on the paintings he wished to share with Lady Sophia and the compelling light he had seen earlier in her eyes.

He found himself unfavourably comparing the forced pleasantries of the evening he was enduring to the interesting and lively conversation he'd enjoyed with Lady Sophia. Somehow, he managed to get through the rest of the evening without going mad. During the carriage ride home, his mother proved yet again that she was totally oblivious to her son's true feelings, for she spoke with considerable excitement about what a fine wife Lady Charlotte Sinclair would make and how they made a perfect couple. Benjamin did not listen, preferring to think of his aunt's upcoming soiree when there would be the possibility of seeing Lady Sophia again.

Chapter 14

Choosing the Perfect Gown

The following day, Sophia joined Lady Helena again for breakfast in the drawing room. She was feeling tired and more than a little miserable. Not because of her brother-in-law's impending visit, which she had actually pushed to the back of her mind, nor the issue of her troublesome finances. The truth was she hadn't slept a lot the night before, for she had been kept awake worrying about what felt to her like a most pressing matter: Attending Lady Margaret's soiree.

She hadn't been to an event like it for a long time, not since before Henry's death, so it felt a little daunting. Lizzie had finished altering the dress and it fitted like a dream, so she had no concerns there. But Sophia was worried about the reaction she would receive to her scar from any other ladies who might be there.

Lady Helena arrived at the townhouse for a late breakfast with Sophia, who took the opportunity to admit her worries to Lady Helena. Her mother-in-law sympathized and told her to forget what others might think of her. They hadn't suffered what Sophia had, she pointed out, adding that, in her opinion, they ought to mind their own business. She suggested that Sophia should rely instead on her own strength of character, and the advice she was being given, of course.

Sophia did her best to take in Lady Helena's advice, which she knew was sensible and intended to be helpful. However, it was not long before her thoughts drifted back to her encounter with Lord Willoughby in Hyde Park the previous day. It was a meeting she knew she would never forget. He had been extremely kind to her, seemingly not taking any notice whatsoever of her scar, and talking at length with her about art. It had all been perfectly wonderful, a reminder that not all the members of the ton were cruel. In fact, in his case, quite the opposite, and it warmed her heart just thinking of him.

After breakfast, the two ladies kissed each other's cheeks affectionately and wished each other a lovely day before they went about their business. Sophia decided to take a walk around the garden of the townhouse, accompanied by Lizzie. As they examined the flower beds, Lord Willoughby once more invaded her mind, especially when they inspected the roses.

The more she thought about him, the more she wanted to know about the man who seemed to be able to see past her scar and into her soul. If she was being completely honest with herself, she was hoping that his aunt's soiree would provide an opportunity for them to get to know each other better. Even if the prospect of facing Society again was filling her with dread and causing her to prevaricate somewhat, she knew she couldn't miss the opportunity of seeing him again. *To see him again, it's worth braving the judgmental ladies of the ton.*

For the rest of the day, with a creeping sense of excitement and dread, she occupied herself with her painting and felt she made good progress. She couldn't help wondering what Lord Willoughby would make of her efforts. She ate a light lunch, with a gothic novel propped open in front of her before returning to her work.

She was just about pack up when Lady Helena called in again, and both of them were delighted to receive an unexpected visit from Beatrice. This made the occasion much more convivial, and the conversation soon turned to what they were all going to wear.

Before too long, all three ladies were gathered upstairs in Sophia's bedchamber. On her mistress's instructions, Lizzie proudly brought out the lilac dress she had altered to fit Sophia. When Lady

Helena and Beatrice gazed at it wordlessly, Sophia found herself becoming upset.

"It's too much isn't it?" she cried, distressed. "I knew it was too soon. I don't know what I was thinking. Put it away, Lizzie, and get out the black one. I shall wear that."

Lizzie looked stricken, and Lady Helena piped up at last. "What are you talking about, dear girl? It's positively splendid. You absolutely must wear it."

"No," said Sophia, her guilt at wanting to wear something other than black had settled over her once more like a blanket. "I can't. I can see you don't approve."

"But Lady Helena's quite right, Sophia," put in Beatrice, frowning at her friend. "Lizzie, do not get out the black again," she commanded the maid, who stopped, looking from one to the other in obvious confusion. "The lilac is perfectly nice and acceptable. You've been in mourning for too long, Sophia."

"But it feels like I'm being disloyal to Henry," Sophia suddenly wailed, overwhelmed by guilt once more. Beatrice rushed up to her and gave her a comforting hug.

"It's all right. This is the first time you've been out into Society for a longtime, and we understand it's daunting for you. But really, it will be all right, and nobody will think any the less of you for wearing half mourning," she told Sophia earnestly. "In fact, by rights, you should really be out of half mourning now too," she added. "Why not wear something pretty? You have lots of lovely gowns, I can see." She gestured at the wardrobe and the racks of dresses hanging there.

"Yes, she certainly has," said Lady Helena, getting up and crossing to riffle through the gowns. "What about this one. This is lovely, and I don't think I recall seeing you wearing it." She held up a gown of pale blue satin with a high waist and wide pink sash.

Sophia looked at it and swallowed hard. "It-it was a present from Henry. It was one of the last things he ever brought for me. I never had the chance to wear it before . . ." She trailed off, staring at the pale-blue dress before adding, "It was one of the few garments which survived the fire."

The dress, she recalled, had been forgotten, left behind in the Dower House when she had moved into the big house after her marriage.

"I cannot wear it. It wouldn't be right," she said, but part of her wanted so badly to wear it, to see the look on Lord Willoughby's face when he saw her in it. She felt torn in two, not knowing what to do.

For once, Lady Helena spoke sharply to her, reminding her that all Henry would want was for her to be happy again. He would not be worrying about the colour of the dress she chose to wear, or that it was one of the last things he had bought for her. It was a beautiful dress, it would suit her perfectly, and it was ideal for wearing to Lady Margaret's soiree.

Nevertheless, feeling under tremendous strain, Sophia persisted with her reluctance, saying in a voice that was filled with disappointment, "I can't go! You'll have to say I'm unwell, I suppose." She then burst into tears, seeing her hopes for a brighter future come to nothing.

However, Lady Helena rose again to the situation, determined to put a stop to what she regarded as her daughter-in-law's senseless behaviour. She told her that she had to return to society at some point. Apart from any other considerations, at twenty-three years of age she was far too young not to do so, and this was the ideal opportunity.

"Sophia, I will not have any more of this. Do you hear me!" Lady Helena spoke sternly, leaning on the authority of age. Sophia stopped crying, and Beatrice started at the older lady, her mouth open. "This is ridiculous. You have already gone well beyond the one year and a day of mourning that was required of you, and enough is enough! Not only that but being constantly dressed in such a drab manner is only serving to make you feel worse, not better! On behalf of my son, whom I knew extremely well and was very close to, I absolutely insist that you wear this gown to Lady Margaret's soiree!" To emphasise her point, she shook the gown on its hanger in fro not Sophie's eyes.

"If you wish to revert to black again after that then I suppose you must," Lady Helena went on, "but only until the modiste can make you some new garments. That old black monstrosity must go! You must realise, it simply isn't your nature, my dear, not to be dressed colourfully."

Lady Helena paused to catch her breath. Not being used to expressing herself quite as strongly as that, she continued more gently. "Sophia, I can't stand by any longer and watch you hurting yourself like this. Filled to the brim with regrets about the past. You must start to live again, my dear. It's time!"

Lady Helena finished by bending over her daughter-in-law to kiss her cheek affectionately.

"Are you sure?" Sophia asked her in a quiet voice.

"Yes, I am!" her mother-in-law cried, her tone putting an end to the matter once and for all.

Soon after that, all three ladies went downstairs for some tea, while Lizzie smiled to herself as she put away the lilac dress and hung the pale-blue gown on the wardrobe door. She just knew that her mistress would make an impression in it at the soiree, and the maid prayed that the person it would impress the most was the kind and gentle Lord Willoughby.

Chapter 15

Benjamin Calls on Sophia

The following morning, Benjamin joined Robert in the lounge of his favourite club. His friend was already seated at the table in a corner, enjoying his first cup of coffee. Since he was also halfway through one of the day's newspapers, he began almost immediately to relay what he had read so far about the latest scandal in the political arena.

Benjamin would usually have listened carefully to him, not wishing to miss anything which they might debate afterwards. But today, he barely heard a word Robert said as he waited for his coffee to be served. Once again, his thoughts were filled with Sophia and their unexpected meeting in the park, which had replayed in his mind over and over again since then.

His train of thought was, however, eventually interrupted by Robert asking him about his dinner at the Sinclair residence. Benjamin sighed loudly at the question.

"I do not wish in the least to talk about my evening at the Sinclairs, except to say it was perfectly dreadful. I do not want to relive the experience over coffee, thank you."

"So, you still haven't proposed to Lady Charlotte, then?" Robert asked, only half teasing. His friend's response was quick and sharp.

"No, I most certainly have not! Nor do I intend to if that's what you are now thinking," Benjamin said, frowning. "Although the way my mother is behaving you would think that I already had."

After conversing for an hour or so, during which Benjamin tried hard to concentrate on the conversation, Robert excused himself. He was expected at his office, he said, to attend to a business matter of some importance with one of his clients. Benjamin felt disappointed as he watched him leave and glanced around the lounge to see if there was anyone else with whom he might converse. Much to his regret there wasn't anyone he knew well enough to approach, which left him feeling restless.

He had not so far been able to decide how to spend his day. He could not see Lady Sophia again, much as he wanted to. It would surely be beyond the realms of propriety to call on her without an invitation, wouldn't it? Miserably, he told himself he ought not to be showing any interest in her at all because of her continuing state of mourning. He did not wish to visit the Academy again, which was where he usually spent much of his time. He felt it would be unbearable, going there without her, especially seeing the landscape again which had appealed to them both, though he still wished he could examine it more closely.

In truth, the only thing he wished was to be in her company. He realised he had been unable to focus on anything else other than her after Robert's departure. Glancing out of the window in despair, he suddenly thought what a beautiful morning it was and how much he would enjoy taking a stroll through the city streets. It was something he didn't usually do. He could even walk along the banks of the Thames, to look at the boats, and the general goings on down there. The fresh air, and bustling activity would help to clear his mind so that he could attend to his own affairs again, he decided. He picked up his hat and left the club.

However, after he had only been walking for several minutes, he came across a young girl selling flowers. Again, all he could think of was Sophia. The beautiful rose she had sketched in Hyde Park sprang to mind, and she had told him that she was intending to paint it when she arrived home. He couldn't help wondering then if she had finished it and how it had turned out. What colours did she have in her paintbox, and which ones had she had chosen to use? Benjamin felt a sudden burning need to view her paintings, but how could he do so, he wondered, without her invitation? And again, there was the matter of her still being in mourning for her husband. It would not be seemly to pursue her, although he had heard that she had no real need to still be in mourning clothes. To him, it showed what a loyal, soulful person she was.

Meanwhile his gaze was on the buckets of flowers on the pavement, which seemed to him to present a work of art themselves, in the colours and textures of their petals and leaves. Nature's art, he was delighted to think to himself.

When he was younger, his mother had insisted he learn the names and meanings of each flower—that language of flowers. Not so much from an educational point of view, but for when it was time for him to give the right flower, with the right message, to a lady. This caused him several more minutes of thought about what exactly he did wish to convey to Lady Sophia Willoughby. He could hardly send her a message that told her she was constantly in his thoughts, and he wished only to spend his days with her, since doing anything else no longer interested him in the least!

In the end, not finding anything with a suitable message, he purchased a pretty bouquet of mixed flowers. He felt sorry for the young flower-seller when he went to pay her, for he thought the girl looked exhausted and not exactly in the best of health. Consequently, he gave her far more money than she had asked for, saying he required no change. He could tell from the look on her face how delighted she was, and felt warm inside to have made her happy.

As he strolled along the pavement, trying to hold the flowers discreetly, he hoped they might at least help to brighten Sophia's day. Without even noticing, he had resolved to call on her at her house, invitation or no. He walked resolutely and quickened his pace as he made his way to the townhouse where she lived. At least, according to his aunt. With his heart pounding inside his chest, he refused to countenance the rights or wrongs of the situation he found himself in. Even though he was unsure how his visit would be received by Sophia, he couldn't get beyond the desire to see her again.

After he arrived at the townhouse, Benjamin was escorted by Soames into the drawing room, where he was left on his own to wait nervously for Lady Sophia. A thousand questions were by this time racing through his mind. Uppermost was naturally whether or not he had done the right thing in calling on her. Perhaps he shouldn't have bought the flowers, but could he have come empty handed? Maybe she really didn't wish to see him? Perhaps he had been mistaken and Lady Sophia didn't feel the connection between them that he did? Maybe she even thought he was boring because he knew he sometimes was, with all his talk about art and history. At least, that was according to Mama.

These questions and others were whirling in his head when the door opened again, startling him. Lady Sophia stepped into the drawing room, a charming smile on her face, and even though she was wearing black, she looked breathtakingly beautiful to him. Benjamin was left at a loss for words for a few moments and had to catch his breath. There was no mistaking the pleasure in her eyes as she smiled warmly at him, and his heart felt it was about to explode with happiness as he realised that she was genuinely pleased to see him.

Sophia was surprised and delighted to see Lord Willoughby standing in her drawing room. She entered, followed by Lizzie, who was carrying some knitting and took a seat in the far corner of the room, a smile playing on her lips.

Sophia noticed the lovely flowers Lord Willoughby was holding out to her.

"Thank you, they are very lovely," she told him, signalling for Lizzie to go and out them in water. However, she suddenly realised that would leave her alone with Lord Willoughby. That was something which could easily be deemed scandalous if it was discovered by the wrong person. But clever Lizzie said quietly that she would leave the door ajar and attend to the flowers as quickly as she could.

Sophia blushed as she politely invited Benjamin to take a seat, which he did, for some reason, in the armchair furthest away from her. Obviously, she realised, he too was sensitive to the fact they were alone and wished to safeguard her reputation. She was embarrassed but grateful for his thoughtfulness. She sat down on the large sofa.

They exchanged greeting and then various pleasantries.

"I do hope you will forgive me, Lady Sophia, for calling without an invitation,2he said. "I had coffee with a friend earlier and was taking a stroll down to the Thames, to enjoy the morning air. Then I came across a flower seller, and naturally thought of your sketch of the rose in the park the other day. You mentioned you intended to turn it into painting. I wondered if you had done so. And if I might see it." There, he had gotten it out.

Their eyes met then, and it was as if the outside world no longer existed for Benjamin, especially when her cheeks flamed crimson. She laughed lightly, a musical sound, and a look of doubt crossed her fine features.

"I, um, I'm not sure I have enough confidence in the quality of my paintings to show them to anyone," she confessed.

"But you are a gifted artist. I am somewhat of an expert in the matter," he told her earnestly. "I could tell instantly from looking at your sketch. I would be enormously obliged if you would humour me and allow me to see some of your canvasses."

"Well, if you really wish to, I suppose." She rose gracefully from her seat and took him out into the hall. There, she showed him two or three of her paintings which hung on the walls. He admired them greatly, noting the delicacy of line and brushwork, enjoying the way it made her blush again. Then, they went back into the drawing room, and she went to fetch the painting he really wanted to see most of all: the rose. It far exceeded any expectations Benjamin had.

"It has all the appearance of delicacy yet with an inner strength," he said, wondering at her artistry. "And the colours and shading you have used is exquisite."

"Thank you, that is very kind," she murmured, her modesty making her even more attractive in his eyes. Then, when they sat down again, to his surprise, she uttered a few words about her husband Henry's interest in art. Once she had begun to speak about it, it was as if a torrent of words had been released which she didn't have any control over, and he listened intently as she spoke, loving the sound of her voice and the passion it contained.

She told him about her late husband's love for the Old Masters, his fascination with how they had painted, and the subjects they chose. She also told him about how they had planned to visit Italy together once the Napoleonic war was over and travel resumed, but they hadn't found the time before his death.

All this was much to Benjamin's amazement, since it almost mirrored his own plans exactly. Unable to believe what was happening, he became a little tongue tied. He could not understanding how Lady Sophia seemed to know his secret thoughts and plans, and they agreed on so much about art too. He found himself telling her that it was his dream to see Pompeii, also the Renaissance paintings in Venice and Florence. Soon, they were so engrossed that neither noticed Lizzie's return until she placed the vase of flowers on the table. The slight sound broke the intensity of the moment, and the conversation faltered.

When Sophia politely offered Benjamin tea, he felt inclined to refuse. He did not wish to outstay his welcome. He rose and bowed low to lady Sophia, thanking her profusely for showing him her paintings, which he very much admired. Lady Sophia curtsied elegantly as he bid him goodbye, and he thought he saw a flash of regret in her eyes, but he could not be sure. Lizzie showed him out.

When he had gone Sophia slumped immediately onto the settee and gratefully accepted Lizzie's offer to bring her a glass of cold lemonade. She felt quite unable to believe what had just happened or to catch her breath. Why on earth had she only seemed to be able to talk about Henry? No wonder Lord Willoughby left soon afterwards, without even a cup of tea.

A tear slid down her cheek. Why do I always have to get everything so wrong? she asked herself, looking around the now empty drawing room.

Chapter 16

A Conversation With Lady Helena

As she sipped the glass of lemonade which Lizzie had brought for her, Sophia began to relive what had just happened. With her thoughts racing, she recalled the exact moment when Lord Willoughby had handed the most beautiful bouquet of flowers to her. As if it hadn't been enough that he had called and brought them for her, his hand had brushed against hers when she had taken them from him, sending a tingling sensation down the full length of her spine. She couldn't explain how it could happen, so soon after Henry's passing, but there was a part of her which was thrilled it had.

In fact, Lord Willoughby's presence in her house felt like one of the most wonderful things to have happened to her. The touch of his skin on hers, albeit accidentally, had made her feel alive again. She certainly couldn't deny that his unexpected visit had brightened her day. If only she hadn't made such a foolish mistake, sending Lizzie out to put the flowers in water, leaving them alone together. Even so, it was a genuine mistake, she quickly reminded herself, trying not to judge herself too harshly. She would never regret the way he had looked at her, which might not have happened had they not been alone.

And for him to discuss art with her again, including her own, had been a dream come true. Of course, he could never replace Henry, but she realised in that moment that she could still enjoy Lord Willoughby's delightful conversation and appreciate his knowledge about art, which for some reason, he appeared to have decided to share with her. Sophia put her arms around herself and hugged herself tightly. She had learned the trick when she felt especially lonely and couldn't bear the feeling any longer, which had recently happened a lot. Now, however, she did it from excitement, and to contain the doubts which were still trying to come to the surface.

Despite the kind words Lord Willoughby had used when admiring her work, she still remained modest about her skill as an artist. But she was also pleasantly surprised by the depth of his knowledge. She found herself appreciating the way he listened to her opinions and the thoughts she expressed. It was as if he did really wish to know them. She hoped with all of her heart that she would see him again at the soiree, reminding herself that he didn't deserve to have to listen to her recollections of Henry, whom he hadn't known.

Instead, she decided, she ought to be drawing him out further on his own opinions and knowledge, in view of the shyness she had sensed beneath his gentle manner. She still couldn't help feeling disappointed when he had taken his leave so quickly. Nor had he left a card with the flowers! She assumed he must simply have forgotten to write one.

Perhaps inspired by Lord Willoughby's favourable appraisal of her work, Benjamin's kindness, Sophia spent the afternoon doing a little more sketching then losing herself in trying to paint the flowers he had given to her. She was soon well into the process of creating a beautiful still life on her fresh canvas, and as she painted, she also considered the meaning behind each of the flowers. He had chosen a delightful mixture of different coloured roses, the brightest blue morning glory, and the paler and more delicate love-in-a-mist.

Taken together they conveyed quite a confusing message. The morning glory meant affection, but love-in-a-mist signified a puzzle him. So, she puzzled him? Whilst pink roses usually meant the start of a relationship, which was obviously another good sign. But this was contradicted by the sprigs of purple lavender, which indicated distrust. The more Sophia stared at them, the more confused she became. She supposed she had hoped they had been chosen to convey a special message to her, but now it appeared

93

they had been chosen at random. That was a little disheartening to her, for it made her wonder if Lord Willoughby cared for her as much as she hoped he did. Unable to solve the puzzle, she decided instead to concentrate on her painting.

As she worked, Sophia felt that all she could do was wait to see what would happen next and, in the meantime, hope for the best. Without intending it, the gold filigree butterfly which Henry had given to her after they were married came into her thoughts then. He had told her that it symbolised Psyche's true love for Cupid. Her heart sank to think of it. She had lost it in the fire. It must have been buried under the fallen timbers and debris in what had been left of the house.

Sophia knew that she would never forget it or her love for him, but she equally knew she couldn't carry on any longer in mourning. She had finally accepted that her dearest Henry wouldn't be coming back. Tears came to her eyes as she looked at Lord Willoughby's flowers and remembered again the kindness he had shown to her when he had called to give them to her. And he never seemed to take any notice of her scar at all. How could she not wish to see him again?

Sophia had just put down her paintbrush, intending to have a break, when she was delighted to see Lady Helena stepping into the drawing room. Her mother-in-law seemed happy. She had spent the day with a friend, she said, and had decided to call on Sophia on her way home. The two ladies embraced each other, and Lady Helena told her about her day.

She remarked that she was delighted to see Sophia painting again. Sophia suspected her mother-in-law attributed the healthy colour of her usually pale cheeks was due to the painting, for she knew nothing of Sophia's thoughts of romance. Nevertheless, while they were sitting side by side on the settee, enjoying the tea and cake which the housemaid had brought for them, Sophia couldn't fail to notice Lady Helena looking curiously at the bouquet of flowers which Lord Willoughby had given to her.

She felt the embarrassment rising to her face, making her cheeks hot. She had no choice other than to reveal that Lord Benjamin Willoughby had called on her and presented the bouquet to her. She felt certain that the confused meaning behind the flowers would not be lost on her mother-in-law, yet she only said how lovely they were. This surprised Sophia, who had half expected her to be upset about it. All of a sudden, Sophia felt another, familiar pang of remorse at the memory of Henry.

"Do you disapprove of my accepting the flowers?" she asked tentatively.

But Lady Helena only reached for her hand and gave it a gentle squeeze.

"It is perfectly acceptable for you to receive flowers from Lord Willoughby, my dear. You are no longer in mourning, and you have done nothing, whatever you may think, to betray dear henry's memory," she said in a reassuring voice.

Sophia felt very grateful to Lady Helena for what she regarded as her kindness and love, and she was glad they were still close. In fact, she noticed that they had been talking more openly with each other than usual. Sophia wondered then if she ought to tell Lady Helena what Henry had said about Vincent, but seeing the contented look on Lady Helena's face, she decided it wasn't the right moment. So, she remained silent, secretly hoping that Henry might have been wrong about his brother being an unscrupulous man.

Chapter 17

Attending Lady Margaret's Soiree

The day of Lady Margaret's soiree finally arrived, and Sophia could feel the butterflies in her stomach as soon as she opened her eyes that morning. After having breakfast, which she could barely eat because of how excited she was feeling, she tried to distract herself with her sketchbook, but without success. Her thoughts continued to drift away from it to the evening ahead. Mostly because of the possibility of seeing Lord Willoughby again.

The day passed slowly until Lady Helena arrived and accompanied Sophia to her bedchamber, where Lizzie was already waiting. Both of them intended to help her get ready for the soiree. As Sophia slipped into her light blue gown, she began to feel a renewed sense of confidence, helped by the many compliments she received from her mother-in-law and Lizzie.

The truth of the matter was that she did look stunning. It was a huge transformation from being dressed head to foot in black, but it was her smile which captivated them both. She looked much more like the earlier version of Sophia they could both recall before tragedy had struck. Her face was filled once again with light and happiness, which, in Lady Helena's opinion, had been absent for far too long. She needed to go out and join the world again, dressed in her old vibrant colours.

Meanwhile, Sophia's joy in wearing such a beautiful gown was contagious. She could barely sit still while Lizzie did her best to remember how to do her mistress's hair in a much more ornate style. She hadn't done it for such a long time that her fingers felt heavy and clumsy, but eventually, she succeeded. When she had finished, Sophia had one last glance at herself in the looking glass, amazed by the transformation in herself, before she pronounced herself ready. After thanking Lizzie for all her hard work, Sophia took Lady Helena's arm, and they went downstairs.

However, before leaving the house, Sophia turned to her mother-in-law and requested a quiet moment to herself. Lady Helena nodded, asking Soames to escort her to the carriage, which he duly did. Sophia went into the drawing room and gazed at the portrait of Henry in its heavy gold frame on the wall. Thankfully, it had also been in the Dower House on the night of the fire, so it had avoided the flames. Lady Helena had insisted afterwards that Sophia must have it.

Sophia whispered quietly to Henry some of the things she wished she could have said to him in person. The, she remained lost in thought for several minutes until she heard Soames coughing politely. Apparently, Lady Helena was eager to leave. Sophia looked at the butler and smiled. She allowed him to escort her out to the carriage. She was very grateful that Lady Margaret had been so considerate as to also invite her mother-in-law to the soiree, so that she would have Lady Helena's support during her first proper outing when she re-entered society.

She was still feeling a little uncomfortable wearing her light blue dress, almost as if they didn't quite belong to her, but she also had the strange feeling that Henry approved. The set of diamonds he had given to her adorned her earlobes and neck, so that her skin appeared to sparkle every time the jewels caught the light.

Sophia began to feel more and more nervous the longer she was in the carriage, despite it only being a short distance to Lady Margaret's residence. Lady Helena smiled at her reassuringly throughout the journey. She recalled how she had felt when she returned to Society on her first outing after her late husband's death. She had imagined that everyone would be staring and whispering about her, as if she was some sort of outsider, or even worse, an oddity. But it hadn't been half so bad as she had expected, she told Sophia, urging her to be positive and try to enjoy herself.

However, despite the reassuring words, by the time the carriage stopped at Lady Margaret's residence, Sophia was almost completely overcome by anxiety. Lady Helena assured her again that everything would be all right. Sophia looked at her mother-in-law and nodded, trying hard to smile before they alighted. Ther were met by the butler, then escorted into the townhouse, where they were warmly greeted by Lady Margaret, who thanked them both for attending her humble soiree.

Lady Helena immediately remarked on how beautiful the room looked.

"I am delighted that you like it. What a job it was! The servants spent all day moving the furniture into the back of the house, then rolling up the carpet before the floor could be chalked to stop anyone from slipping. I had quite forgotten the extent of it, but I did so wish to have a little soiree this evening, though it's only be a small affair for family and friends," Lady Margaret said, looking around with concern, adding, "I do hope we have enough seats for everyone."

While the two older ladies continued to converse about practical matters, Sophia stood quietly next to Lady Helena. Her eyes were instantly drawn to a painting of Lord Willoughby and his father on the opposite wall, which she couldn't help but admire. She stared at it for perhaps a little too long, she realised, for her interest began to attract the attention of two other ladies who were nearby whom she didn't know.

Lady Margaret also noticed Sophia looking intently at the painting and remarked on the likeness between her brother and nephew. She added that the pair were alike in many ways, quite different, of course, to Lord Willoughby's mother. She snorted in

98

distaste as she mentioned Lady Rosamund, which made Sophia wonder about the lady herself.

As more guests began to arrive, it was not long before Sophia began to imagine that she was being stared at, that people were resenting and objecting to her presence among them because of her scar. She took a grip on herself, telling herself quite firmly that she shouldn't take any notice, as Lady Helena had recommended. However, it was difficult to convince herself, and she was relieved when Beatrice appeared. She was accompanied by James and her mother. Once she was with her friends, Sophia felt a lot better, and her confidence began to return.

Her heart skipped a beat when the door opened, and her eyes met those of Lord Benjamin Willoughby as he escorted his mother into the drawing room. After that, all she could see was him.

Chapter 18

Lady Rosamund Willoughby is Angry

As Benjamin escorted his mother into Lady Margaret's drawing room, he was thrilled to see Lady Sophia standing on the other side of it. Once their eyes met, neither of them wished to or could look away. But the sweetness of the moment was soon broken by Lady Rosamund, who gave a horrified gasp. Immediately, he realised she had seen Lady Sophia and quickly noted that he was staring at her. Despite his joy at seeing Lady Sophia, his heart sank, knowing the trouble his mother could cause if she wished to, with her fixation on his marrying Lady Charlotte Sinclair.

"Margaret, I cannot believe you have been so foolish as to invite such a repulsive person to the soiree. No one wants to see someone like that at the best of times, so why should you think Polite Society would wish to socialise with her? You really have excelled yourself on this occasion by entering the realms of stupidity!" Her stage whisper could be heard by almost everyone in the room, including Lady Sophia and Lady Helena.

Benjamin paled. He couldn't believe how ill-mannered his mother was being and couldn't fail to notice the stares they were now receiving because of her loud outburst. He was ashamed to be escorting her, knowing he would by implication be associated with her appalling behaviour and opinions. He also noticed that one or two of the older ladies who had heard what Lady Rosamund had said seemed to be nodding in approval and didn't appear in the least to object to what she had said about Lady Sophia.

Nevertheless, as far as Benjamin was concerned it really was the final straw. Without further ado, he dropped his mother's arm, leaving her to her own devices. This drew a stunned gasp from those closest to them for what they perceived was his rudeness and ill treatment of his dear mama. When he made his way across the drawing room, he could feel Lady Rosamund's eyes boring into his back as she glared angrily at him. He knew she was alert to the damage he might well have caused to her otherwise excellent reputation by shaming her so in public. If the scandal sheets got hold of such a juicy titbit of gossip, they would have a field day.

Lady Margaret, who had also moved deliberately away from her sister-in-law after her outburst, was smiling at her nephew as he approached the group she and Lady Sophia had joined. Nephew and aunt exchanged warm greetings. But the fullness of Benjamin's smile was for Lady Sophia alone, whom he complimented immediately on her lovely, pale-blue dress, causing her cheeks to redden delightfully. Benjamin wasn't quite able at first to believe the transformation in her appearance, and how the shade of blue was the perfect colour for her. In his opinion, it was obvious his mother's description of Sophia as repulsive was not only untruthful, it was also absolutely despicable.

However, Benjamin wasn't oblivious to the hushed murmurings and peculiar glances being cast in their direction. In that moment, all he felt was a strong urge to protect Lady Sophia Montgomery, for whom he had by now developed the most enormous respect. He was quite unable to understand how the ton could be so cruel to her, a young woman who had already suffered considerably. Most of the guests didn't even know the person behind the scars, and he wanted none of it!

Lord Benjamin Willoughby raised himself up to his full height as he continued to happily converse with Lady Sophia, and every eye in his aunt's drawing room was fixed on them. His intention was that Sophia wouldn't feel alone with him at her side, or, at the very least, quite so intimidated. He could tell she felt reassured by his presence, and he wasn't going to leave her, notwithstanding any intervention from his mother, or anyone else for that matter. What he was doing now was the right and honourable way to behave, to the best of his knowledge and belief, and he was ready to face the consequences of his actions.

However, it soon became evident that Lady Rosamund didn't intend to give up quite so easily. Apparently further incensed by

Lady Margaret smiling benevolently at the scarred widow and Benjamin as they conversed, she stalked, unescorted, across what was to be the dancefloor, almost slipping in one place where the chalk on the floor appeared to be missing.

She joined the group, making a point of completely ignoring Sophia, interrupting her midsentence as she was speaking to Benjamin. She then made a further spectacle of herself by grabbing Benjamin's arm and telling him in a voice which invited no argument that there were some nice people she would very much like him to meet. However, at that precise moment, the small orchestra played a chord to indicate that the evening's first dance set was about to begin.

Benjamin gently but firmly removed his mother's hand from his arm as he smiled at Lady Sophia. Trying to ignore his mother and make it appear as if there had simply been a misunderstanding, he gallantly asked her if he might have the honour of dancing with her. Lady Sophia's elegant brows flew up, and she looked astonished at the invitation. Then, she smiled warmly at him and politely accepted his request. As they took their positions on the dance floor, Benjamin couldn't help noticing his mother glaring at him disapprovingly, but he found he cared not a jot.

Chapter 19

Sophia Dances with Lord Willoughby

Sophia's heart was racing as she felt every eye in the drawing room on them when she took Lord Willoughby's hand and stepped onto the dance floor with him. It really is a dream come, she thought, thoroughly enjoying twirling around the floor in his capable arms. She soon found herself lost in the eyes of the man she knew by now that she was falling in love with. His gentleness made her feel protected, even cherished, and he was a wonderfully light-footed dancer too. Despite his mother being so terribly rude, Sophia's heart soared, for she had not felt so happy in a long time.

After the dance set, Benjamin escorted Sophia to the refreshment table, where they soon began an animated conversation about art. She admired the portrait of him and his uncle, saying she thought it exceptional. This caused them both to blush and then laugh at their own embarrassment. However, despite her enjoyment of his company and their interesting conversation, Sophia soon realised that some of the other guests were staring in their direction. What was more, the looks were not all kind. Gradually the murmuring among these guests intensified until she could eventually hear their words. They spoke of the shameless audacity of her behaviour, that a widow with a scar didn't have any right to return to Society, and certainly not to look for a match with an eligible bachelor such as the rich and handsome as Lord Benjamin Willoughby!

Sophia made the mistake of glancing away from him as she tried to see who was saying such dreadful things about her. She saw Lady Rosamund glaring at her with a look of fury on her face. Realising the reason behind Sophia's sudden stiffening in his arms, Lord Willoughby whispered to her that she shouldn't worry about what anyone else might think. Sophia tried to do as he suggested, but the poisonous words wounded her deeply.

Just then, however, they were joined by Lady Helena, who ably accomplished her own round of magnificent staring at the main offenders, including Benjamin's mother. Her looks defied anyone to persist in such atrocious behaviour, or they would face the wrath of her tongue. This caused the majority to quickly turn away and act as if they were guilty of nothing. Sophia felt strengthened by her support, which was soon bolstered by the arrival of Beatrice and James, whose presence alongside her spoke volumes of their disdain of this unfair treatment of Sophia.

James immediately began a conversation with Benjamin about a painting he had recently seen at the Royal Academy. He wished to learn his friend's views about the artist, who wasn't as yet well known. Meanwhile, Beatrice had taken Sophia to one side, and over glasses of lemonade, told her friend how delighted she was to see her in the arms of one of the kindest gentlemen she knew.

For Sophia, this immediately refuted her lingering suspicion that she was, by her actions, betraying Henry's memory. Beatrice was adamant that Henry would never have denied the woman he loved a second chance at love. All he would have wanted was Sophia's happiness, she was certain of it. She insisted that Sophia mustn't let such negative thoughts, or anything else for that matter, destroy her chances of happiness with Lord Willoughby.

In any event, and as Lady Margaret had intended, the evening ended early, with none of the entertainments which often took place at a soiree after the dancing had finished. Sophia felt the loss when she had to bid Lord Willoughby goodnight, and she noticed how reluctant he too seemed at their parting. His mother, however, cast Sophia dark looks as they left, which left Sophia with serious misgivings. It was only Lord Willoughby's smile that kept her from fleeing.

Lady Helena invited Sophia to accompany her into her townhouse for a night cap when the carriage arrived in the street where they both lived. As they entered the house, they had no idea that a surprise awaited them in the drawing room.

They entered the drawing room together, unpinning their hats, to be faced with a man who resembled Henry so greatly, that both stopped in their tracks, open mouthed, to stare at him.

"Vincent!" Lady Rosamund cried out, while Sophia stood in confusion, finally realising that the man before them was her long-lost brother-in-law. Lady Rosamund approached him, and the pair embraced. When it came to Sophia's turn, she was about to speak to him when she noticed he was scrutinising her appearance in a way that made her feel very uncomfortable. However, he greeted her warmly, asking after her health, and finished by saying how delighted he was to see them both.

"I apologise for arriving at such a late hour and without giving any notice," he told them. "Especially since I appreciate how tired you ladies must be after your evening out." He spoke quite pointedly, and Sophia felt the familiar pang of guilt at the implication she was somehow betraying Henry by attending a social event.

"I shan't keep you up, but I shall return in the morning, if that is convenient, Mama, and we can catch up over breakfast," Vincent suggested.

"Of course, dear," his mother declared, dabbing at her eyes with a hanky.

"I have many questions to ask you about your progress after the loss of my dear brother," Vincent said, "and I'm ready to answer questions you may wish to ask me."

With the arrangements to meet at breakfast made, Sophia observed Vincent closely as he spoke further to his emotional mother. She couldn't deny that he appeared outwardly genuinely remorseful for his absence and the loss of his brother. In fact, he was kind and considerate in his manner. So much so that when Sophia announced her wish to return to her home, he declared it was his duty to escort her himself.

Sophia hesitated to accept, but she was unable to detect any artifice in his features, so she took his proffered arm and listened to his many pleasantries as they walked the few steps along the street to her townhouse. He then waited to bid her goodnight until she had been safely admitted by Soames. All of this gave Sophia the impression that he cared very much about her safety and wellbeing.

Sophia soon retired to her bedchamber, where Lizzie helped her undress and put on her nightgown. She wanted to hear all about the soiree, so Sophia, still distracted by Vincent's sudden arrival in their lives, told her as best she could, leaving out the bits about the cruel remarks and instead saying how much she had enjoyed dancing with Lord Willoughby, who had been kindness itself.

As Sophia eventually drifted off to sleep, her mind was consumed with thoughts of Lord Willoughby, and a happy future with him which she hadn't dared to believe might be possible. Her mind rejected Lady Rosamund's rude behaviour and that of some of the other guests. Instead, she focused on Lady Helena giving her blessing to her during the carriage ride home and Beatrice whispering in her ear how delighted she was to see that Lord Willoughby was taking a serious interest in her. James had apparently said that he knew Lord Willoughby Benjamin very well, and he truly was the kindest and nicest gentleman one could hope to meet. Apart from her late husband and himself, he had apparently added, with a grin on his face.

After a night of tossing and turning in bed while thinking constantly of Benjamin, Sophia found it difficult to open her eyes the following morning when Lizzie tried to rouse her with a cup of tea. Consequently, she arrived a little late for breakfast at her mother-in-law's townhouse. Vincent and Lady Helena were already seated at the table. Her brother-in-law was still eating a hearty meal of bacon, eggs, and kidneys. Lady Helena was having a much lighter meal of a small piece of bread and a single rasher of bacon, professing not to be very hungry.

Both welcomed Sophia warmly after she apologised profusely for her lateness. This prompted Vincent to politely remark that it was entirely his fault for having kept them both up so late the previous evening.

While Sophia was served with her breakfast, Lady Helena said that she had already informed Vincent of Mr. Blackwood's report on her financial situation. At that point, he looked at Sophia with what appeared to be considerable concern before putting down his knife and fork to address her.

"My dear Sophia," he began, clearing his throat, "we have known each other for a long time, and I am aware that we continue to share a love of my dear brother Henry, may he rest in peace. So, I wish now to reassure you that, although there was a slight misunderstanding between us in the past, which I deeply regret, you have nothing to fear from me. As your only living male relative, and the same goes for my dear Mama, I am here now to accept my responsibilities. I fully intend, to the best of my ability, to act as a protector and guide to you both. Please think of me now as the head of this family, as I know from our conversation last night that my dear Mama sees it that way," he said, pausing to smile magnanimously at Lady Helena before his eyes turned back to Sophia, was listening intently.

"I will be making arrangements forthwith to take on Henry's title, since I know that he and my father would wish me to act without delay. This will allow me to ensure the well-being of both my mother, and you, Sophia. I wish to care for you both in the way I would very much like to."

Sophia noticed that Lady Helena was smiling at her son as if he truly was the answer to her prayers, but there was still something which didn't seem quite right to Sophia. Memories of the boy she had grown up with came to mind. She recalled how manipulative Vincent could be, and how his mood could quickly change. Did all these promises and undertakings to act in their interests really mean that he had changed for the better? She simply wasn't sure. But despite her misgivings, she smiled at them

107

both, wishing to try her best to give him a chance to prove himself. However, her optimism came with a caveat that told her she would be best advised to see what actually transpired before she fully endorsed her brother-in-law's actions.

Only time would tell if Vincent really had changed for the better, she told herself. After all, what harm could it do if Lady Helena had told him about the lawyer's opinion of her finances? Mr Blackwood must surely be wrong. With a little further guidance, he would, she felt certain, be prepared to report that he had made a foolish mistake. Maybe Vincent was the right person to give him that guidance.

Truthfully, Sophia was aware that her feelings for Lord Willoughby were growing stronger by the minute and prevented her from thinking too long or in any great depth about anything else. They soon made her forget her concerns over Vincent as she absentmindedly ate her breakfast and replayed in her mind how wonderful it had been dancing with Lord Willoughby . . . and how she wished for a repeat of it as soon as possible.

Chapter 20

Lord Willoughby's Betrayal

Benjamin had left his bedchamber early and was sitting behind the desk in his study deep in thought. He had been unable to stop thinking about Lady Sophia, how beautiful she was and how much he enjoyed her company. He tried his best not to allow the confrontation with his mother to spoil the enjoyment he was taking from his thoughts. At the same time, he was not looking forward to the aftermath which he knew was be inevitable.

He knew from his aunt that Lady Rosamund had left her sister-in-law's residence on the previous evening in a fit of fury that her youngest son was guilty of what she perceived to be no less than a betrayal. Incensed by such defiance on his part, she hadn't announced her intention to leave or even said goodbye to him. His aunt had strongly advised him to leave his mother to her own devices before he even considered talking to her about his obvious interest in Lady Sophia Montgomery. That, she said, would at least give him the opportunity to speak to her more calmly and avoid an irrevocable situation which might occur in the heat of the moment.

Benjamin groaned. There really wasn't any way of avoiding this battle of wills with his mother. Whilst not wishing in any way to upset her, he had accepted that this was something he would have to follow through despite the consequences. His father had always said that a gentleman needed to pick his battles wisely and that it wasn't necessary to fight on every single occasion. Benjamin firmly believed that this foolish argument with his mother ought to fall into the latter category. Except that this time he would have to remain strong, as he would not only be acting as peacemaker but fighting for the woman he loved. He wanted to protect Sophia, but also ensure she could remain at his side. He would not be coerced into a ridiculous sham of a marriage with Lady Charlotte Sinclair, whom he wasn't sure he even liked. It was only natural that he should be entitled to love whom he pleased. For that reason, if no other, he decided he was right to regard his mother's matchmaking as at the very least misguided. Although the fact remained and, as his father had learned if what Benjamin had seen of his handling of Lady Rosamund was the measure of it, the dispute with his mother would require him doing as little as possible to fuel the flames of their conflict.

The simple fact remained that he was unable now to deny the attraction he felt for lady Sophia, nor did he wish to do so. Neither did he see any good reason why he should, especially now she was no longer in mourning. Benjamin had instead become even more determined to spend more time with her. He wished to see her again as soon as he possibly could, and so he decided on the spur of the moment to invite her to an upcoming painting exhibition he had been thinking about going to. Without further ado, smiling to himself, he picked up his pen with the intention of writing the invitation, his heart racing in excited anticipation of seeing Lady Sophia Montgomery again.

However, this pleasant activity was soon interrupted by the sudden arrival of his mother, who burst unannounced into the study. Startled, Benjamin looked up in alarm, his daydream of Lady Sophia shattered. Lady Rosamund's eyes flashed with intense anger of a sort which Benjamin couldn't recall having seen in her before. She reprimanded him severely for dancing with Lady Sophia at the soiree, referring to her disparagingly as "that woman". In her tirade, she also called Sophia "the scarred widow", pointing out to Benjamin that it was quite beyond her comprehension how he had been able to hold the woman's hand, let alone be so close when dancing with someone as repulsive as her!

Finally, in a flourish, she insisted that he come to his senses and start courting Lady Charlotte Sinclair. That was, she pointed out, if he hadn't been quite so foolish as to already lose his chance with her despite all of the effort his mother had put in to guide him and smooth the path for a romance. Lady Rosamund stamped her foot in temper and glared at him as she harangued him. With venom in her voice, she told her youngest son that he had better comply with her wishes or suffer the direst of consequences. She insisted that she was not prepared to allow him to disgrace the family name any further with his appalling behaviour.

Although Benjamin was more than a little shocked by the extent of his mother's anger on this occasion, he was soon reminded of the respect he had for Lady Sophia, his admiration and, yes, his love for her. Though he was well aware that he could stand up and defend his actions, he chose to remain silent. He knew full well from past experience that when his mother got herself into one of her fits of rage, it was best not to argue with her. Moreover, it would be a pointless exercise, since she would continue to believe she was right whatever he said.

Instead, he waited until she had flounced out of his study before he picked up his pen again, to finish off writing the invitation he had started. He tried to put out of his mind the horrific descriptions his mother had unjustly used when referring to Lady Sophia's scar. He knew they must have caused her considerable pain to hear. At that point, Benjamin came to the conclusion that not only was his mother insufferable, but he sometimes didn't care for her very much. He had no idea how she could treat someone as gentle as Sophia was in such an unkind manner, without showing any compassion for her whatsoever. It made his blood run cold.

Later that day, still trying to shake off the effect his mother's intrusion had had on his equilibrium, Benjamin met Robert for drinks at their club. He had hoped that conversing with his friend would help to take his mind off the confrontation. Although he still wasn't prepared in the least to comply with her wishes and found it difficult to forgive her verbal attack on Sophia, he equally didn't enjoy being responsible for upsetting his mother, nor being involved in a confrontation of any description.

On the spur of the moment, Benjamin started to reveal what had happened that morning, simply in response to Robert asking him what was wrong. He did not realise until too late that he would now be obliged to also tell him of the interest he had in Lady Sophia. But he didn't feel comfortable discussing his innermost feelings with anyone, not even his best friend. And so, it wasn't long before Robert was grinning in delight and congratulating Benjamin on finally finding a love match. He stood up from the table, almost causing their glasses of wine to spill in his haste to slap Benjamin heartily on the back as a means of evidencing his friend's success.

He then revealing that he had been misled by Benjamin's absentminded manner, which had made him believe that he was, in fact, in love with Lady Charlotte Sinclair. Benjamin spluttered into his wine to hear this misconception and was about to object strenuously to it until he was reminded that it didn't matter because he didn't care for her in the least. He actually found himself laughing over it, along with Robert.

However, after the two gentlemen had become calmer and talked about the situation over coffee, Robert revealed that although he didn't know the man personally, he had recently seen the Vincent Montgomery was back in town. He had to explain to Benjamin, who did now know, that Vincent had apparently been estranged from both Sophia's husband and his family due to his underhand behaviour. He was also known to still have a string of debts, with a number of creditors actively seeking repayment.

Benjamin sipped his wine thoughtfully. Robert's revelation had left him feeling unsettled. He knew that as a widow without the protection of a father or brother, and seemingly only having Lady Helena Montgomery at her side, this left Sophia in a highly vulnerable position. Especially if, in light of what Robert had told him, her brother-in-law might not be the gentleman he presented himself as. Benjamin's heart sank. Just when he had thought everything was going as well as it could in his relationship with Sophia, apart, of course, from his mother's interference by, he couldn't help wondering how Vincent Montgomery's return might affect their potential romance. It could even cause complications in their friendship. Maybe Mam will get her wish after all, he thought bitterly. For might not Vincent now exert sufficient influence on Sophia to put a stop to them even meeting?

Even though he remained at heart a gentle soul, Benjamin knew he would do everything in his power to rise to the challenge. He was fully prepared to fight for the right to love Lady Sophia Montgomery if it came to it. Admittedly, it would be one of the most important battles of his life, and it was one that he couldn't possibly countenance losing.

Chapter 21

Sophia Doubts Vincent Montgomery's Intentions

Later that day, Sophia was in the drawing room with Beatrice, who had decided to call on her. Apparently, she said, she hadn't been able to think of anything else other than Lord Benjamin Willoughby's interest in her best friend after she had learned of it at Lady Margaret's soiree. The two ladies were having tea and nibbling slices of Cook's excellent carrot cake.

Dispensing with their usual few minutes of pleasantries due to their mutual excitement, they were intently discussing the development of what Beatrice had insisted was Sophia and Benjamin's romance. Sophia was greatly encouraged that Beatrice was so clearly excited by the news. It was yet another endorsement that she was not doing anything wrong and was entitled to seek happiness once more. It was heartening to hear Beatrice declare that, as far as she was concerned, it was exactly what Sophia needed.

She wanted to know the basis of their connection, which prompted an admission from Sophia that they shared a passionate interest in art and painting. When Beatrice cajoled her into telling her more, Sophia admitted that they also shared a love of Nature. Beatrice then asked how many times they had met and where, making Sophia laugh as she recalled their first encounter at the Royal Academy, then that they had met by accident at the modiste's shop. Sophia admitted that had been a special moment for her, for it was when she had taken in the fact that he appeared not to care a jot for her scar and talked to her like a human being, without staring at it. This, she told Beatrice, had been confirmed during their talk at Hyde Park.

The truth of the matter was, though, she admitted to her friend, everything had been happening so fast. She truly felt as if she had been swept off her feet by Lord Willoughby, especially after he had asked her to dance at the soiree. Despite all of the unpleasantness which had been going on around them and, of course, the love she had for Henry, it had been one of the happiest times of her life. She thanked Beatrice sincerely for the part she had played in bringing them together. She then made Batrice squeal in delight by admitting that she believed she was falling in love with Lord Willoughby.

After the two ladies calmed themselves, they became quietly engaged in a conversation about Vincent's arrival, the news of which had surprised Beatrice.

"I still can't believe that he simply turned up unexpectedly, so late in the evening. Such an inconvenient time when you must both have been exhausted! What on earth was he thinking doing such a thing?" she asked indignantly. "Lady Helena might well have been on her own. How could he have been so certain that you would also be there, Sophia? From what you have told me, it was quite by chance. I know he is a part of your family, but that surely isn't any excuse to behave in such an ill-mannered and inconsiderate way. His visit could easily have waited until the morning. I am only saying this because of my concern for Lady Helena and you, you understand."

Beatrice hesitated, seeing Sophia's furrowed brow. Then, she asked tentatively, "Do you think your brother-in-law can be trusted?"

Sophia understood at once what she meant. "Oh, Bea, I just don't know. I am so confused. It's been on my mind since I found out that he was intending to visit us. But I feel so disloyal in even questioning Vincent's honesty, for he is Henry's brother. But I do know that even my late husband found him difficult. Vincent was always the same as a boy; he could be so impetuous, acting

115

without any real thought, but also intent on getting his own way, even if it hurt others' feelings. You never knew from one minute to the next how he would react.

"However, after he wrote to Lady Helena recently, I decided to wait and see if he had changed after he arrived." Sophia broke off, sighing heavily before continuing. "The problem is, apart from the strange manner of his arrival, he has been charming and considerate. He seems to be full of remorse for being absent from our lives for such a long time, but then again, I also have the distinct feeling that something isn't quite right with him, but I just cannot put my finger on it."

Sophia paused, looking at Beatrice as she gathered her thoughts. "It concerns me that I don't know the exact reason for his estrangement years ago, nor why Lady Helena hasn't talked about it. Unless, that is, she felt it was something better left in the past. As I don't really know what to make of it, I've been trying to think instead of what Henry would say. And that makes me think I ought to give Vincent a chance, especially when it's what Lady Helena appears to want."

Beatrice looked at her friend with concern. "I just hope he doesn't try to interfere between you and Lord Willoughby, she said, and was about to say more when they were interrupted by the appearance of Soames. The butler was holding a silver salver, on which there lay a letter addressed to Sophia. Sophia felt her heart begin to race, and the butterflies in her stomach fluttered as she opened it. She felt the blood rush to her cheeks in delight to discover it was an invitation from Lord Willoughby to attend an art exhibition with him the following day.

"What is it?" Beatrice asked, and Sophia handed her the invitation, her heart brimming with excitement. "Oh, marvellous! You see, he is serious about you, whatever that awful mother of his says," her friend immediately declared after reading it, her eyes twinkling.

"I can hardly believe it," Sophia sighed, her hand to her chest. "I never thought that Lady Margaret's soiree would be the start of a real romance between us. My life so far had been filled with so much tragedy, but here is proof that I have a chance at finding happiness again!"

"Well, isn't that what I've been telling you all this time, you silly goose?!" Beatrice told her as the pair embraced warmly.

Sophia had been disappointed that he hadn't called on her earlier, but he did seem to be quite shy. Maybe that was the reason for his earlier reticence. His earlier confusion concerning the bouquet of mixed flowers he had given to her also showed that he wasn't used to situations like this. She tried not to think again of what his mother's reaction had been to them dancing.

Irrespective of all that, what mattered was that Lord Benjamin Willoughby was showing an interest in her. It was as if the sunlight coming in through the windows of the drawing room had suddenly become much brighter. After reading the invitation again to make certain she wasn't mistaken about it, she smiled once again at Beatrice and asked the question that was now uppermost in her mind.

"But what about his mother? She obviously hates me," she said, her happiness fading a little. "The way she glared at me, and the unkind things she said at the soiree."

An image of Lady Rosamund's furious face came quite clearly into Sophia's mind, and her heart sank.

"Ladies like her think I shouldn't be allowed out in pubic to socialise because of my scar," she told Beatrice, her hand moved involuntarily to her face.

Beatrice looked dismayed but said, "Take no notice of her. She likely wants him to marry someone of her choosing, and that's why she was so mean to you. But he's old enough to make his own decisions. She'll get used to it over time."

She was about to reach out to Sophia again to comfort her when the door opened, and they were interrupted by the arrival of Vincent. He came swaggering into the room as if it belonged to him. When he saw them, he straightened up and greeted them, bowing politely to them both.

"I do apologise profusely for interrupting your tea and conversation. I have just paid a visit to my mother and, since it is so near, I thought I would drop in to see my delightful sister-in-law again."

This made Sophia to blush, and she was caught off guard when he said, "May I enquire as to what you were talking about?"

Sophia hesitated for a moment before replying. "Oh, nothing important." She remembered her manners then. "Would like to join us for some tea and cake?" Secretly, she hoped he would say no.

"Thank you, I most certainly would," he boomed, to her consternation, sitting down near them. She rang for more refreshments to be brought.

Whilst they waited for the housemaid to replenish the tea and carrot cake, the trio engaged in exchanging bland pleasantries. However, it soon became clear to Sophia that he had an agenda that did not include time wasted on small talk. As soon as the maid had served them and left the drawing room, he repeated his original question about what they had been discussing before his arrival.

Realising she was obliged to tell him of her affairs, now that he was head of the household, Sophia revealed that she had been invited to attend an art exhibition. She was greatly surprised when Vincent offered immediately to escort her to the event, professing a deep interest in art. This was an even greater surprise to Sophia, along with names of the painters he briefly mentioned, none of whom she had heard of. It seemed that Vincent had developed this interest since they had last met.

Once again, there was something about the way he talked about the topic that didn't sit quite right with Sophia. He had never once shown any interest in her painting before, or in Henry's passion for art. If the truth be told, he had sometimes appeared to ridicule what he regarded as them both wasting their lives on such nonsense. Presumably, she thought, he wishes for that to be forgotten. And it made her suspicious.

With a despairing look at Beatrice, Sophia tried to politely refuse his offer to escort her to the exhibition, fearing her outing with Lord Willoughby was about to be spoiled. And she was proved right because when Vincent absolutely insisted on accompanying her, good manners decreed that she was obliged to reluctantly accept. She could only hope that his presence wouldn't disrupt a single moment of the precious time she would have with Lord Willoughby. But a part of her knew that it probably would.

Then, seemingly having done what he intended in asserting his presence in Sophia's life and affairs, it wasn't long before Vincent took his leave.

Once Vincent had left the drawing room and the two ladies were alone again, without the threat of being overheard or indeed disturbed, Beatrice immediately warned Sophia to be careful of Vincent.

"He seems to be trying far too hard to ingratiate himself and appear to be nice," she observed.

"I know, I feel exactly the same. Ever since I heard of it, I suspected that Vincent's return would cause trouble, for me and his mother," Sophia confessed, her happiness at Lord Willoughby's invitation now thoroughly replaced by a deep sense of misgiving

119

about her brother-in-law's motives that she simply could not shake.

Chapter 22

A Difficult Day for Benjamin

The following day, Benjamin arrived early at the art exhibition. His heart was pounding hard inside his chest after he his rapid walk to the hall, unable as he was to contain his excitement at the prospect of seeing Sophia again. Nevertheless, as he stepped inside the building, he couldn't fail to be instantly captivated by the artwork on display. He slowly made his way along the nearest row of paintings, admiring each canvas, but all the while watching out of the corner of his eye for Sophia's arrival.

His heart missed a beat when he caught sight of her. Sophia was dressed in a beautiful, pale lilac gown, with an embroidered bodice, and a pretty bonnet to match. She looked absolutely stunning. The bodice had a drawstring beneath it which accentuated her neat silhouette, and the coral beads she wore around her neck completed the outfit perfectly. She was completely out of mourning, and he was thrilled to discover her true appearance when she was able to dress how she pleased. Her veil was also nowhere in sight, and he did not even see her scar as he took in the delicate beauty of her features.

When he approached her, Benjamin was surprised and dismayed to discover that Sophia wasn't alone. He had expected her to be with her maid. But it wasn't Lizzie who was accompanying her, but another gentleman whom he didn't know. His heart sank. She surely didn't have another suitor, did she? It would be the height of poor manners to bring him along to an event when she had been invited to it by someone else. Lord Willoughby raised himself up to his full height. He simply couldn't believe that Sophia would do something as cruel as that, and he wished to find out the truth. She was making her way towards him with a smile, closely followed by the strange gentleman, who didn't look at all as pleased to see him as she did.

As soon as Sophia was close enough for him to see properly, her eyes told Benjamin the truth. He saw he had been foolish to worry that he might have lost her to someone else. Her gaze quickly melted into his own when she looked into his eyes. He sensed her unease when she introduced him to her brother-in-law, Vincent Montgomery.

Benjamin greeted the man politely, but that didn't stop him from considering other reasons for the man acting as her escort, none of which appealed to him in the least. The most obvious one was that he had an interest in his late brother's wife himself. That or he intended to prevent her from remarrying a man whom he had not approved. Either would, presumably, suit his own purposes. Given what Robert had told him regarding Vincent's questionable reputation and character, Benjamin would not put anything past the man, and he soon came to share Sophia's obvious unease.

As they slowly walked up and down the galleries, looking at the paintings, Benjamin couldn't help but be alarmed when he realised that Vincent was staring mostly at Sophia and himself rather than the paintings, which he only glanced at quickly. This left Benjamin feeling even more uneasy about the man's possible intentions. However, it wasn't long before Benjamin's attention was focused completely on Sophia, sharing in her delight when she exclaimed over the different paintings she liked and they explored the exhibition together.

It was not long, however, before Benjamin saw that Vincent had decided to make his presence felt, interrupting their conversation by speaking to Sophia in a loud voice, so that the other visitors to the exhibition took note. He asked her opinion on individual paintings, telling her specifically what he liked or disliked about each one. By doing so, to Benjamin's annoyance, he prevented them from talking about the niceties of brush strokes, technique, and colour.

In the meantime, Vincent completely ignored Benjamin, who therefore had plenty of opportunity to form the view that, despite his assertions to the contrary, Sophia's brother-in-law didn't actually know a great deal about art. If anything at all. Moreover, judging by some of the nonsensical and disparaging remarks he made about various works, he often clearly misunderstood the artist's interpretation of the subject matter.

Recalling then his decision to fight for Sophia, who didn't seem in the least to be enjoying these intense exchanges with her brother-in-law, he deliberately interrupted Vincent when he was in mid-flow, giving his opinions on an Italian master's work. He claiming to have seen it during his travels through Spain, presumably mistaking the Italian artist's name as being Spanish. When Sophia voiced her surprise and asked him when he had been in Spain, Vincent replied shockingly that things like that weren't any of her concern, and that she didn't need to know his personal business.

Benjamin was appalled by this, and his hackles rose at once. Sophia's question had been innocent enough, and only someone with something to hide would have reacted in such a way. Benjamin knew it was contrary to the person Vincent was clearly attempting to portray. The tone in his voice had changed to a belittling, unpleasant one. Furthermore, his reprimand made Sophia blush from clear surprise and embarrassment.

Although Benjamin hadn't intended to intervene, at least not yet, since they were in a public place, his urge to protect Sophia remained strong. He also couldn't help but notice how she had moved closer to him, as if she was afraid or at least wary of her brother-in-law.

"Come now, Sir, perhaps you will tell me then?" he said, a hard tone in his own voice when he spoke to Vincent directly. "My understanding is that the painting hasn't yet been shown in Spain. The painter was an Italian who lived in Florence, and this is the first time his work has been exhibited abroad," Benjamin added, staring at the man. He wished to show Vincent quite clearly that he was behaving like a fool and that his treatment of Sophia was unacceptable.

But to his surprise, Vincent seemed unconcerned by being challenged in defence of his sister-in-law. Benjamin assumed it was because, as both of them knew, Vincent ultimately had the upper hand so far as she was concerned, being her only living male relative.

"I am sorry to say it is you, Sir, who is mistaken. I most definitely viewed this painting when I was in Madrid," Vincent said brazenly, with a smile that didn't reach his eyes, which were now like pieces of flint, though his tone of voice was perfectly reasonable.

His response added weight to Benjamin's earlier opinion that Vincent's response to Sophia's question wasn't a simple case of him being mistaken about the painting. It was an outright lie, clearly told to further his own aim of appearing more knowledgeable than he was about art. If the man was prepared to lie about something as inconsequential as seeing a painting in a country where Benjamin knew for certain it hadn't been displayed, he would presumably be able to tell lies just as easily about much more serious matters.

Lord Willoughby knew then that Sophia could be in danger. However, she had put her hand gently on his arm, and her eyes were imploring him not to enter into an argument with her brother-in-law. So, he reluctantly backed down. At least, for the time being, but that in no way meant he had relinquished his desire to love and care for her. There had to be a way to deal with Vincent Montgomery, but all he could presently do was hope that he would soon be able to find it.

For the rest of their visit, Benjamin remained silent and was obliged to listen to Vincent's inane conversation with Sophia, which he continued to lead. Benjamin knew her knowledge of the majority of the paintings was far greater than her brother-in-law's, sensing that she obviously felt obliged to remain largely silent too and defer to his purportedly much greater knowledge.

When they returned to the entrance of the exhibition, there occurred another awkward moment when Benjamin took his leave of Sophia. She appeared noticeably upset by the turn of events, her eyes appealing to him before he was obliged to watch her walk away on her brother-in-law's arm. He practically boiled with fury as he walked to his carriage, resenting Vincent's unwarranted familiarity with her and the way he had spoiled their time together.

As he walked to his club to meet Robert for coffee, Benjamin's anger changed to intense disappointment that seeing Sophia again hadn't turned out as he hoped. He had wanted it to bring them even closer together. He tried his best to think instead about the paintings he had seen but couldn't succeed in distracting himself. His concern about Vincent's dishonourable intentions was too great. He decided to tell Robert everything, as his old friend would never betray his confidence. So, once they were comfortably seated at their club, in a quiet corner, where they could speak discreetly without being overheard, that was exactly what he did.

Robert was equally dismayed when Benjamin told him what had happened at the exhibition. Without further ado he offered to look into Vincent Montgomery's background, to ascertain if he could uncover any possible hidden motives for his unexpected return to the family. Robert had innumerable connections in London and across the world, so he would be able to make such enquiries much more easily than Benjamin.

Benjamin accepted with alacrity, for he was grateful for any help his friend could give him.

"I don't see any other way forward, unless I abandon my courtship of Sophia, and I'm not about to do that, I assure you!"

Feeling as if his day couldn't get any worse, Benjamin eventually had to leave Robert to attend a family dinner, where his mother once again acted as matchmaker. Throughout the entire evening, she attempted to force Lady Charlotte Sinclair into his arms. He did his duty as good manners demanded, but all he could think of was holding Sophia as they danced at his aunt's soiree, and how wonderful it had felt to be so close to her.

In truth, the hours at the dinner passed in somewhat of a blur for Benjamin, who hardly paid any mind to his mother's machinations. His thoughts continued to dwell on Sophia, more specifically, his concern regarding Vincent Montgomery's intrusion in their lives. He couldn't help but wonder whether she was being forced right now to sit opposite the ill-mannered buffoon at the dinner table and make polite conversation when she didn't wish to. More importantly, Benjamin agonised over what designs Vincent had on her. He recalled how beautiful Sophia had looked that morning at the exhibition, and he couldn't believe that Vincent, or any other man for that matter, wouldn't be interested in her.

Benjamin endured sitting next to Lady Charlotte once more at dinner, politely feigning interest in her vapid chatter. All the time, he was imagining how different the evening would have been if Sophia was at his side. It was so easy to converse with her on their shared interests. He bristled to think how much more enjoyable the exhibition would have been if they had been attending it without the uninvited presence of her brother-in-law. His heart became consumed with jealousy again at the notion, and he couldn't help but wonder again whether Sophia and Vincent were dining together that evening. She should be here with me, he thought bitterly, looking accusingly across at his mother.

Lady Charlotte's voice droned on in the background. She was telling him about some gossip she had read in the scandal sheets. Apparently, a disgraced viscount was being sent to the debtor's prison for not paying his creditors. She clearly blamed the unfortunate gentleman, whom Benjamin knew had lost his fortune through no fault of his own. When Benjamin took the trouble to explain to her what had actually happened, she would have none of it. She showed no compassion or even interest in the fact that the gentleman's investments and business, being mainly based in France, had been all but wiped out because of the Napoleonic war. Although she did listen politely enough to his explanation, she went on to tell him that the scandal sheets were truthful and that he must surely be mistaken!

Benjamin knew then without a doubt that he had to get away from Lady Charlotte Sinclair and his mother's continual meddling, whatever it took. Something had to change, and quickly. It was always going to be Sophia whom he wished to marry and have at his side for the rest of his life.

Chapter 23

Dinner at the Stanhope Residence

The following morning, Sophia woke up with a headache. She still felt overwhelmed by what had happened at the art exhibition and couldn't get beyond the thought that she had no idea when she would see Lord Willoughby again, if ever. They should have had such a wonderful time. He had gone to the trouble of finding an exhibition she would ordinarily have loved, and there had been so much she wanted to ask him about the paintings. She hung her head in shame. What must he have thought about her being accompanied by her brother-in-law. The way Vincent had behaved was appalling. Henry would never have spoken to her like that, and she also knew in heart neither would Lord Willoughby. Her cheeks flushed bright red when she thought of how magnificently he had defended her, and how he had backed down again when he saw it was what she wanted him to do.

It was all Vincent's fault! Not even knowing that something like this would happen, she had still been instinctively afraid of the damage he could cause. Now, she didn't even know if Lord Willoughby would even wish to see her again. The hot tears which slid down her cheeks did nothing to cool them, nor the headache pounding at her temples. She was too afraid to think about what could have been the cause of her brother-in-law's behaviour yesterday, nor what more she might expect from him in future. It didn't appear that he had changed at all, and that he was now putting on an act, to appear as a seemingly honourable and kind gentleman. That was clearly far from the truth, she decided, with no small bitterness. Even worse, he had quickly slipped back into his pretence without any difficulty, becoming the perfect gentleman during the carriage ride home. He had expressed concern for her comfort, talking pleasantly of inconsequential matters once they had left the paintings, and Lord Wiloughby, behind.

Sophia pulled the coverlet further up, trying to hide herself under it. That was how Lizzie found her when she brought a cup of tea into the bedchamber. The tea did help to revive Sophia somewhat. So much so, that despite her feelings about Vincent's behaviour that day before, she was able to cherish the few minutes she had shared with Lord Willoughby when they were looking at the paintings together, before Vincent had so rudely interrupted them. All she could hope now was that Lord Willoughby realised and understood the difficult position Vincent had placed her in by inviting himself to the exhibition, without her being able to explain this directly to him.

It was important that he should know that her feelings for him hadn't changed, and how much she appreciated him coming to her defence. He really was the gentlest and kindest of men. Sophia wished then that she had been able to convey all of that to him and more the day before, but when he had taken his leave of her, it had still been under Vincent's watchful gaze. She recalled then how her brother-in-law hadn't taken his eyes off them, not even for a second! Another tear slid silently down her cheek when she began to doubt that she would ever see Benjamin again.

She rallied herself, and Lizzie helped her to dress before she went downstairs for breakfast, though she had no appetite. As she stepped into the drawing room, she was surprised to find Lady Helena had arrived unexpectedly and was seated at the table on her own drinking tea. She told Sophia that Vincent had gone out early to attend to some important business. Not wishing to spend the morning alone, Lady Helena had decided to call on Sophia to sit with her, as she had often done in the past when they were both trying to come to terms with Henry's loss.

Soames knocked politely on the door while they were eating, to deliver a letter from Lady Beatrice Stanhope. Sophia opened it eagerly, wondering what her friend had to say, and, somewhat irrationally, if she had news of Lord Willoughby. However, it transpired that both Lady Helena and she had been invited to an informal dinner that evening held by Beatrice's mother, Lady Clara Stanhope. Sophia guessed that Beatrice, knowing nothing about what had happened at the exhibition yesterday, had persuaded her mother to hold the event with the sole intention of promoting the budding romance between Lord Willoughby and Sophia.

Sophia replied to Beatrice as soon she and Lady Helena left the breakfast table, as they both wished to attend. She asked Soames to arrange for her reply to be sent immediately. Then, she immersed herself in painting, while lady Helena produced a piece of crochet work from her bag and began to work on it.. Both of the ladies were quite happy to carry on with their own pursuits in companiable silence, taking comfort from being in the same room as each other.

Sophia had not considered Vincent when they had discussed the invitation from Lady Stanhope. They had become used to socialising without him, and he wasn't as yet a constant part of their lives. He came and went as he chose, without any indication of his movements or a time of return. Sophia hoped that Lady Helena hadn't also received a similar rebuke from him when asking questions about his movements as she had at the exhibition.

However, by the time they were ready to leave for the dinner that evening, he still hadn't returned. This allowed Sophia and Lady Helena to take a carriage to the Stanhope residence without him having the opportunity of insisting that he should also attend the dinner.

Sophia had decided once again to wear one of her favourite gowns from before she went into mourning. Lady Helena gave her instant approval as soon as she saw the pretty white dress she knew Henry had loved. It had the palest of pink flowers embroidered on the skirt and ribbons of the same colour on the bodice. She told Sophia that she looked beautiful, and that she would make a wonderful impression at the dinner. Her knowing look told Sophia that her mother-in-law was referring to Lord Willoughby, and she smiled at her, grateful as always for the older woman's support.

During the carriage ride, Lady Helena tentatively brought up the subject of Vincent.

" I do hope his reappearance won't cause a rift between us, dear. You know I value your love and friendship much too highly to allow that to happen," she said, somewhat mystifyingly. Then, looking thoughtful, she added, "I wish he wasn't been quite so secretive, though. That much about him hasn't changed. But I hope he will be able to sort out the true state of your finances with Mr Blackwood. He must have a greater understanding of these things than either of us."

"Yes, I hope so too, but he has said nothing of it as yet," Sophia replied. "I suppose he is very busy."

"I am not sure, but I suppose he is busying himself in trying to sort out the transfer of Henry's title. He will get around to it, dear. I am confident that he has changed his ways and will be a great help to us in the future," Lady Helena said.

But Sophia didn't think she looked convinced at all, and she was not prepared to agree with her mother-in-law's assessment of Vincent after his behaviour at the exhibition. Nor was she about to give Vincent the benefit of the doubt, but she decided it was not the time to find fault with him. She had no wish to hurt her mother-in-law or spoil the evening ahead by distressing her. She hadn't mentioned anything at all about the exhibition earlier in the day to Lady Helena, only telling her that she had enjoyed viewing the paintings when she had asked. Since it seemed unlikely that Vincent would tell his mother about his appalling behaviour, Sophia decided it would be diplomatic not to mention it.

Any further conversation between them was interrupted by the carriage coming to a halt. Sophia and Lady Helena were soon greeted by the Stanhope family's butler, who escorted them into the drawing room, where they were warmly received by Beatrice and her husband. Beatrice's mother, Lady Clara, welcomed them warmly, clearly delighted to see Sophia. The group was exchanging pleasantries when the butler announced the arrival of Lord Benjamin Willoughby and his aunt Lady Margaret Lancaster.

Sophia couldn't help it! Her heart missed a beat when she saw Lord Willoughby walk in, and she thrilled to see the look of affection in his eyes as he greeted her. She could not stop smiling at him, and as soon as their eyes met, it was as if the drawing room fell silently into oblivion. They were in their own little world, where only true love prevailed.

Chapter 24

Wishing for More

Benjamin felt the emptiness inside his heart begin to thaw as soon as he saw her. The warmth and tenderness in Sophia's eyes reached out to him, and it was impossible for him not to see the depth of emotion within them. Regardless of their circumstances, he hadn't lost her after all. It was also much to his delight that only Lady Helena appeared to be accompanying her. There was no sign whatsoever of Vincent Montgomery!

Nevertheless, Benjamin knew that didn't mean he wouldn't simply turn up later, no doubt completely ignoring the fact that it would be very bad manners to do so. Hopefully, however, it wouldn't be too long before Robert discovered the truth about the man, thereby placing Benjamin in a much better position to protect Sophia should she need it. As for the present, without wishing to waste even a single second of any of the time they had together, Benjamin quickly approached her. He bowed, and she curtsied, smiling as he placed the softest of kisses onto her gloved hand when he lowered his lips to it. He did his best to convey in his manner of greeting the depth of his feelings for her.

When he looked up at Sophia's face, her cheeks had flushed a deep crimson, as if she was completely overcome by his gesture. He became aware then that they weren't alone, however much they might wish to be, and Benjamin made an effort to recover from the effect which seeing her again had on him. Propriety returned to his thoughts, and he finally released some of the intensity of the moment by starting to exchange pleasantries with her. All the while, he was entranced by her beauty and charm, as well as her proximity, which made it tempting to simply take her in his arms and kiss her soundly on the lips!

When the butler announced that dinner was ready to be served, Benjamin immediately offered his arm to Sophia to escort her into the dining room. His heart filled with pride when she graciously accepted, and he felt the warmth of her arm tucked in his. But the time it took for them to walk side by side to the dinner table was brief, and she soon had to let go of his arm. The loss felt unbearable to him. However, once they were seated next to each other at the dinner table, nothing prevented them from enjoying each other's company. They began to relax, and the conversation between them flowed naturally.

As they waited for the soup to be served, they shared their thoughts with each other. Benjamin secretly wished they could talk more openly about the last time they had met at the exhibition, and more so what was now happening between them, but he was aware that there was the distinct possibility that they would be overheard by the Ladies Helena and Margaret, who were seated opposite. Consequently, it wasn't long before their conversation inevitably turned into a discussion about various artists and their work.

Benjamin was glad to be able to guide Sophia because of his greater knowledge and experience of the field. He had already thought that if he should be fortunate enough to see her again, he would like to introduce her to some of the painters he had discovered because of his association with the Royal Academy, and also from attending lectures in London. Eventually, he asked her if she had come across the work of Albrecht Durer, whose early paintings included some wonderful landscapes, he explained, and who had later moved onto other parts of the natural world when choosing his subject matter.

"I have heard of him, Lord Willoughby, but I haven't yet had the opportunity to study his work," Sophia said, somewhat breathlessly he noticed when he accidentally moved his hand closer to hers. delighted by her reaction, he nevertheless moved his hand slightly away from hers and began to tell her more about Albrecht Durer. He became so carried away in sharing the details of Durer's life and work with her, that he inadvertently slipped into the conversation then that the artist had apparently abandoned his wife on their honeymoon, so that he could go on a painting expedition. This caused Sophia to blush enchantingly, prompting him to declare that he would, of course, do no such thing if he had recently married!

134

Fortunately, they were saved from further embarrassment by the arrival of the soup, which they both began to eat immediately. A little later, when they happened to glance at each other in the same instant, both of them burst out laughing. Seeing the humour in their shared discomfort had only served to make them feel closer to each other, which pleased Benjamin hugely. After that, he found it easy to resume their conversation about Durer and describe some of his paintings to Sophia which he thought she might like. He included his particular favourites, the delicately done landscapes and still lives with flowers and animals. He told her that Durer's portraits were equally stunning, as were his rendering of his subjects' hands, for which he had a fascination. To his satisfaction, Sophia appeared to be happily drawn into the world which Benjamin's words and passion for art was creating for her.

Benjamin paused to catch his breath at this point. He was delighted to be able to share his passion with Sophia, who was very receptive, and he felt alive just seeing her reactions as he described the paintings of Durer. Once again, it seemed to him as if there were only the two of them at the table, with everything, and everyone else, fading into the background.

Sophia seemed absorbed in what he was telling her, watching him with admiration in her eyes as she listened to him speak. His heart swelled when she eventually said she would try to find as much information about Durer as she could in the books at the circulating library. She told him with enthusiasm that she very much wished to see the paintings for herself which he had described and learn more about them, from the point of view of the artist's technique and use of colour.

Benjamin found himself becoming even more captivated by Sophia's intellect and her insight into his observations. Her thoughts and opinions were both fascinating and refreshing, and he couldn't help comparing her intelligent remarks to Lady Charlotte's recent comments about the scandal sheets. Lady Charlotte did not come out of it well. As the evening progressed, he found it increasingly difficult to tear his gaze away from Sophia. He was struck by the realisation that his feelings for her were

135

growing deeper than he had ever imagined possible despite them not having known each other for very long.

During their animated conversation about art, he also couldn't help but glance at her scar. He marvelled once again at the strength and resilience it represented, a symbol of all that she had already suffered in her short life. Lady Sophia Montgomery truly was a remarkable woman, and he hoped once again with all of his heart that she would stay in his life. For without her, his would be empty.

As the dinner drew to a close and the last of the desserts were being eaten, Benjamin was filled with a sense of contentment that he hadn't experienced for a long time. His heart felt much lighter than it usually did, and his was mind clearer. Moreover, he knew with absolute certainty that Sophia was the reason for this newfound happiness.

The more he gazed at her beneath the candlelight from the chandelier above, he longed not only for more moments like this but also the opportunity to deepen their connection to each other.

Chapter 25

Benjamin Must Obey his Mother

The following day Benjamin was in his study, struggling to concentrate on the book he was reading, while he sat in what had once been his father's armchair. The was trying to push from his thoughts the letters which he ought to have been replying to, some of which now required his urgent attention. It didn't really matter what he tried to do, for he was unable to concentrate. He was completely lost in thoughts of Sophia, their shared love of art, and the way she had looked at him last night when he had been talking about it. He had hoped that his book about Albrecht Durer might distract him. It still contained a lot more information he didn't know. But all it had done was make him realise even more that he couldn't wait to speak to her again and tell her what he had discovered.

Feeling quite overwhelmed by these thoughts, if not a little exhausted, since he had barely slept after returning home the previous evening, Benjamin decided on the spur of the moment that he had to see Sophia immediately. Nothing else would do! He threw the book down onto the table next to the armchair and stood up, intending to call on her. However, before he could get any further, his heart sank as he heard his mother's voice coming from the hallway. It was clear she was in the process of pushing past his butler after arriving unexpectedly and was on her way determinedly to the study.

It wasn't long before Lady Rosamund had pushed the door of Benjamin's study wide open in her haste to speak to him. Also, without any form of greeting whatsoever or preamble, she informed her son that she wished him to be Lady Charlotte Sinclair's escort during the promenade hour later that day. It was the sole reason for her call, and she didn't need him to make any excuses. In her opinion, which she had no difficulty whatsoever in voicing, Benjamin had so far been far too slow in pursuing his courtship of Lady Charlotte, whom she must remind him was a great beauty and extremely wealthy. Whilst his courtship of her, if it could even be described as such, had reached the point of having become almost non-existent. Again, in her opinion, this most certainly wouldn't do!

Benjamin looked at his mother in despair, and his heart sank even further inside his chest. Just when he had plucked up the courage to go and see Sophia, which was what he wanted most of all to do, the moment of confrontation with his mother he had been avoiding had arrived. Doing his best to muster the energy to deal with it, he realised the only way to go about it was to be honest with her.

So, he cleared his throat, and said, "I am sorry to have to say this again, Mama, but I will. Please, listen to me this time. I can't do as you ask or, believe me, I would. It has never been my intention to hurt you, nor will it ever be, but what you are asking is impossible. I simply have no desire to pursue Charlotte Sinclair, and . . ."

Benjamin hesitated before he felt able to continue, knowing that what he was about to say would add more fuel to the flames, which he could tell were already burning fiercely inside his mother's heart.

"I have even less now. Because I have discovered that I have an interest in someone else!" he said quickly, so that the words would be gone from him, and he would have at least said them. There it was! He had told her, and now, he watched to see how she would react. Although deep in his heart he knew exactly how it would be and that he was right to fear the worst.

Rosamund's expression had darkened, and she replied immediately.

"You dare to say this to me, Benjamin. After all I have done for you and know far better than you do about matters of the heart. I sincerely hope I am wrong, but I can't help but be afraid that this newfound interest is in the scarred widow you couldn't seem to take your eyes off the other evening!"

Much to Benjamin's dismay, Lady Rosamund then proceeded to give him a stern lecture on how a courtship with Lady Sophia Montgomery would ruin his family's reputation and was not at all what his late father would have wanted. She struck him with her words as brutally and deeply as an axe by invoking her late husband's memory. Benjamin felt the fullness of her disapproval and was not left in any doubt whatsoever of the intensity of her feelings on the matter.

If it hadn't been so serious, he might have considered it bizarre that someone could go to such reprehensible lengths to achieve what they desired. She was prepared to even go so far as destroying her own son's chance of happiness, submitting him to a life of misery with a wife who didn't share or have any interest whatsoever in his passion for art. That alone made him feel bereft. Even worse, of course, would be the ultimate loss of Sophia. How his own mother could countenance so much destruction felt far beyond him in that particular moment. So much so that Benjamin slumped into his father's armchair, with the misery he felt clearly etched on his face.

Lady Rosamund glared at him then for good effect, to reinforce the point she had made before she flounced out of the study. She left her son deep in thought, especially concerning his own foolishness in hoping that the situation would improve. It now seemed that his mother was forcing him to take sides, so that it would be either a case of losing Sophia or her. She doubtlessly did not believe she would lose such a contest. Why couldn't she simply see sense? But Benjamin knew with a feeling of dread that the situation had gone too far, especially now his mother knew about his interest in Sophia.

Benjamin groaned. There really wasn't any way in the world he felt able to stop his relationship with Sophia from developing. Nevertheless, he realised it might not be the right time to call on her, given the upheaval within him his mother's visit had caused. He decided reluctantly to postpone his visit and picked up his book again with a heavy heart, quite unable to concentrate on the paintings within it.

The image of Sophia's smiling face and her eyes gazing into his own the previous night was all that he could see. It made him realise even more strongly than before that he could never willingly give her up.

Chapter 26

Losing Lord Willoughby's Love

Meanwhile, feeling inspired by her conversation with Benjamin and what he had said about Albrecht Durer's versatility as an artist, Sophia was fully immersed in a new painting. It was a little different to her usual style since she wished now to try and stretch her existing skills. She was attempting to capture the garish quality of some of the city streets onto the canvas. She recalled again what Benjamin had said about the strengths and weaknesses of his preferred painters, how they had developed their craft and learned from each other, or by trial and error.

His enthusiasm had made her keen to try different things. This current painting would, hopefully, go some way to stretching her imagination and skill in the use of colour and light. She knew now that they could be different in all of her paintings, depending on the mood she wished to evoke in the subject matter and the people looking at her work. None of which she had been thinking of before, when she had simply painted what she felt like once she picked up her brush.

She thought again of how she had felt when going shopping with Beatrice after their visit to the modiste's shop, which had resulted in her yearning to be in Nature. So, instead of using a bright, sunny day to depict one of the London streets they had visited, as she had been originally intending to do, she began trying to portray it differently to reflect the feeling she had when she was there. She wanted dark clouds and rain, the best match for her mood at the time, when she had been growing tired, but it was proving to be a lot more difficult than she had imagined. Despite concentrating fully on the canvas, and what she had seen that day, she soon discovered there would be a lot of trial and error involved in getting the painting to look as she wished it to.

Her thoughts also continued to drift from time to time to the dinner last night when she had sat next to Lord Willoughby. She realised now what an important role in her life he was playing and that she very much wanted it to continue. Their conversations had even started to help her develop as an artist, which made her smile happily to herself. Life was definitely changing, and for the better. However, her concentration was soon interrupted when, much to her surprise, Mr Blackwood, arrived at the house.

According to Soames, it was apparently for a private meeting with Mr. Montgomery. Sophia felt flummoxed. Why hadn't her brother-in-law mentioned it? As it was, she didn't know what to do, other than to instruct Soames to ask Mr Blackwood to wait in the parlour. He was to offer him tea, on the understanding that she would speak to him shortly. She intended to run upstairs to change into a clean day dress since the old dress she was wearing was daubed with paint. However, she also wished to finish the section of sky she had been working on before Soames interrupted her, and she decided to do it quickly before going upstairs.

While she worked, she tried to push any concerns about Vincent's motives in arranging the meeting without informing her to the back of her mind. She felt he had no right to ask Mr Blackwood to come to her house, not without at least telling her his intention to do so. She also wondered if Vincent intended to ask her to attend the meeting once he had arrived. It was all most peculiar, she thought, frowning, for it wasn't as if he had been living in her house. Beset by a sense of dread for what might be about to happen next, she realised with dismay that Vincent was already showing signs that he regarded her property as his own, which was obviously unacceptable. It seemed too far of a stretch of her imagination to consider that this predicament was simply the result of a simple omission on his part.

Continuing to feel dismayed, Sophia carried on with her painting as quickly as she could. Even after she overheard Vincent arriving, Soames didn't come in to tell her that the two gentlemen required her attendance at their meeting, though one might have thought they would since it concerned her finances. Not having experienced a situation like it, nor having the benefit of any other guidance, she didn't know what to do. Her mother-in-law was intending to visit one of her friends that morning, and she recalled with a pang of anxiety that Henry could also no longer help her. Even as Lord Willoughby's name and the image of his face came to her, she tried to dismiss it. She couldn't possibly ask him to become involved in her personal affairs or intervene in what was a family matter. As much as she would like to have done. Could she?

After what must have been nearly an hour, with Sophia still lost in thought, Soames returned to say that the two gentlemen had gone. When Sophia asked him why he hadn't let her know that Mr Montgomery had also arrived, Soames became very concerned, if not a little distressed. It transpired from his explanation that Vincent had assured him there was no need to disturb Her Ladyship, as she already knew all about the meeting and wouldn't be attending it.

Sophia decided not to gainsay what was a blatant lie on the part of her brother-in-law and thereby create an even more difficult situation which the innocent Soames had inadvertently been caught up in. This was especially the case as the butler then said that Lady Rosamund Willoughby was waiting to speak to her as a matter of urgency.

At that point, Sophia was caught completely off guard by Lady Rosamund, who had clearly decided not to wait any longer, rudely stepping into her drawing room. Sophia was, of course, still wearing her painting dress and would have liked to have the opportunity to quickly change before she received any other unexpected visitors. Especially Lord Willoughby's objectionable mother, who had been so nasty to her the last time they had met. She wasn't entirely certain that she wished to be in her company at all, at least, not without Lady Helena or Lord Willoughby being present. However, that clearly wasn't an option, for a very determined looking Lady Rosamund was already inside the drawing

143

room, waiting to be asked to take a seat, completely ignoring the fact that she had intruded on Sophia's privacy in her own home.

Sophia however remembered her manners and quickly asked Soames to bring them tea if Her Ladyship would like a cup. Her Ladyship declined, saying that her business with Lady Montgomery would only take a few minutes. Lady Rosamund's tone of voice was icy, and when she glared at her again, Sophia could feel her stomach churning.

She was hardly able to believe that something so awful was happening to her. First, there had been Vincent's appalling behaviour, and now it was being closely followed by what was obviously going to be a confrontation with Lord Willoughby's mother. Feeling the tears pricking behind her eyelids, Sophia resolutely held them back, determined not to give Lady Rosamund the satisfaction of making her cry.

In any event it wasn't long before her visitor made the reason for her call perfectly clear. Adopting a cold, and calculating manner, her words were insistent and cruel.

"I intend to speak to you quite plainly, Lady Montgomery," she said without further ado. "Despite the persistence of your intentions, a successful courtship with my son is out of the question! You surely must realise that Benjamin deserves much better than someone like you. Look at yourself in the glass if you are in any doubt about it. You are already a widow, and badly scarred to boot!" She paused to smirk unpleasantly at Sophia. "It must cease, right now. Do you hear me? Your ongoing interest is causing Benjamin to neglect the pursuance of a romance which would be better suited to his character and position."

Lady Rosamund words dripped with scorn as she continuing to stare at Sophia's scar pointedly. Sophia was on the verge of her tears, but the woman continued haranguing her mercilessly.

"I don't expect someone like you to understand, and I have come to you today solely out of a mother's love for her child. I tell you, let Benjamin go. It is something which you would readily do if you truly cared for him."

The final words hit Sophia hard, and she struggled to keep her composure. Her heart was aching at the thought of losing Benjamin and the love she believed was growing between them. But Lady Rosamund had sowed the seeds of doubt in her mind. Her self-esteem and confidence were already fragile because of her disfigurement. As a result, Sophia began to question herself as to whether there might be a grain of truth in what Lady Rosamund was saying. As harsh and unpleasant as it might be to accept, if she did indeed love Benjamin and she believed she did, then would she not want the best for him, as his mother had pointed out so clearly?

In addition to that, she felt the pinch of jealousy, wondering who the lady was in this other romance his mother had mentioned. Was Benjamin involved with someone else too besides her?

She had no time to gather her thoughts or reply to Lady Rosmund, for the lady rose and left abruptly, without feeling the need to resort to any pleasantries. Sophia was left to grapple with her emotions, feeling very shaken and unsure of the right path to follow.

She sat on the settee for a long time afterwards, mulling over what had happened. Until, with a heavy heart, she decided it would be best to let Benjamin go, however much she didn't want to and however much heartache and pain it would cause her. She did not want the situation to become even worse should Benjamin come to realise later what he had done in associating with a woman like her. No doubt, he would be reminded constantly by Lady Rosamund that he had chosen someone who didn't have any right to expect a romance with a gentleman of his status and position. Somehow, she would persuade him that he couldn't truly love Sophia because she had a prominent scar on her face and could never be considered a good match for him.

A life with Benjamin had come to mean so much to Sophia, but in her heart, she knew she had to do whatever it might take to preserve his future happiness. Lord Benjamin Willoughby, whom she had grown to love as the man with the kindest eyes, was also very handsome. Lady Rosamund was right! He did deserve so much better than her.

Chapter 27

Two Broken Hearts

The following day, Benjamin decided to call on Sophia without any further ado. Despite his mother's attempts to stop him from seeing her again, he was missing her far too much not to do so. Having thought about his predicament constantly since his mother had barged into his study the day before, he had come to the conclusion that it would be a good idea to offer to escort Sophia on a walk through Hyde Park.

This would not only give them the opportunity to speak to each other again, but to simply be in each other's company and regain the closeness he craved. Also, he hoped that it would help him clear his head of any lingering unpleasantness. Although it was obvious that the damage to his relationship with his mother had been done, he wasn't entirely certain that it could, on this occasion, be repaired. Especially not since he had with considerable determination not complied with her wish that he should escort Lady Charlotte during yesterday's promenade hour afternoon.

Just to be near Sophia again was what he now craved the most. He knew in his heart that it would be impossible for him not to continue getting to know her better. How could he stop now, when he had finally found the woman whom he had only previously been able to dream of? No! It was out of the question. He had decided to take his book about Albrecht Durer with him, so Sophia could see for herself the beautiful landscapes, flowers, and animals in the paintings he had told her about. If she wished to, they could find a quiet bench in the park and look at it there.

It wasn't long before Benjamin found himself at Sophia's townhouse, with the book safely tucked under his arm, and her butler had escorted him into the drawing room. Much to his dismay however, he sensed immediately that something wasn't right. After he greeted her warmly, Sophia averted her eyes almost immediately. Her manner seemed strangely cold and distant, as if she had, for some reason, withdrawn her affection from him. But why? Benjamin couldn't help feeling confused and equally alarmed. It wasn't the reception he had expected. He immediately began to explore in his thoughts what he had said to her and how he had acted when they last met. He blamed himself straight away for the change, but nothing came to mind that could reasonably be the cause of it. In fact, quite the contrary. His own recollections of the dinner at the Stanhope residence had all been very positive, and he had been certain Sophia felt the same.

Nevertheless, it seemed to him now that her usual warmth and openness had been replaced by a quiet restraint. Thankfully, however, not before he had glimpsed the shadow of tenderness in her eyes before she looked away. It gave him a glimmer of hope that whatever had caused the sudden change in her might still be overcome. But this thought wasn't sufficient to combat his confusion and the stutter returned to his voice when he asked her if he could escort her to the park.

Sophia's refusal to accept what she described as his kind invitation, again, definitely wasn't what he had expected, despite the change in her demeanour. Even more so when she went on to say, with a pained expression on her face, and what he still believed was love haunting her eyes, that it would be best if they didn't see each other again. Benjamin felt stunned. It was as if she had delivered a blow from which he might not recover, so strong had his feelings for her become.

Along with the urgency of his desire to love and protect her, at the cost of any detriment to himself, it was impossible for him to readily accept this sudden change in her.

"But why? What has happened?" he asked, without wishing to pressurise her in any way, but equally unable to simply comply when it seemed as if he was on the point of losing her. It was too important not to at least ask the question. "I don't understand," he said finally, trying to explain his persistence to her in his confusion.

"I'm sorry, Benjamin, especially if I caused you in any way to mistake my intentions regarding our friendship. I don't wish to enter into the romance I believe you are looking for," Sophia replied, in a listless tone of voice. "It simply wouldn't work, Lord Willoughby. I can't discuss it any further with you. I am deeply sorry, but if you respect me, you will take your leave now."

Sophia's words cut through Benjamin to the core. Feeling completely bereft, he was left with no other choice but to depart since that was what she said she wished him to do. But he still couldn't believe it was the truth. Something definitely wasn't right! Sophia, whose hand he had kissed tenderly and seen the look of love in her eyes throughout their last meeting, had turned against him, without any proper explanation for it. It simply didn't make any sense, especially not after her warm and loving manner towards him the last time they had met. Moreover, it was also apparent that what she had just done had caused her considerable pain, if the pallor of her skin and the haunted look in her eyes were the measure of it.

Unable to retrieve his book, which he had quietly put on her table next to her paints, and feeling unable in any event to do so, he turned his back and walked out of the drawing room. He did not see her face crumple in distress or hear the anguished cry which she deadened with a hand across her mouth when she saw him leaving. If he had, he would have gone to her immediately and taken her in his arms, regardless of social etiquette. He would have insisted that she explained to him what was wrong.

Nevertheless, despite Benjamin not being able at the time to imagine that it was possible, the situation was about to become even more unbearable. He was collecting his hat from Soames, who was trying his best to look impartial when he also couldn't believe that Lord Willoughby, for whom he had the utmost regard, was already taking his leave after only a few minutes of being in her ladyship's company, when Vincent Montgomery knocked on the front door and was admitted to the hallway by the footman. He seemed completely at his ease, as if he had every right to be there. Benjamin gave him the merest nod in response to his greeting, whilst the man's surly features only added to Benjamin's unease. It left him in no doubt whatsoever that something was clearly amiss, increasing his reluctance to leave. He couldn't help hoping that Sophia wasn't in any danger. Moreover, if she was, that Vincent wasn't at the root of it. It was, though, very easy to believe that there was something highly disreputable and unpleasant about him.

With this still in mind, he was glad that he had already arranged to meet Robert later for drinks at their club. It gave him the opportunity to discuss his sadness and bewilderment at Sophia's rejection and his ongoing concerns about the return of her brother-in-law. He was grateful when Robert told him what he had so far been able to discover about Vincent Montgomery. Namely, that there were strong rumours circulating in the most reputable of circles about his mounting debts and questionable affairs. For most of his adult life, it would appear that Vincent was known to have been associating with what might be described as the wrong sort of gentlemen. It was generally accepted that not only was he unscrupulous but also completely ruthless when it suited his purposes. Essentially, money meant everything to him, and he didn't seem to care in the least how he got it.

Robert added his own feelings then, saying that whatever Vincent was up to now so far as Lady Montgomery was concerned, it was unlikely to be a legitimate dealing and would most likely be to her detriment. However, he said he would need to dig deeper to discover exactly what that could be. Benjamin could evaluate then whether he was in a position to come to her assistance, and if so, act accordingly. All of which only served to heighten Benjamin's suspicions and alarm. He wondered if Vincent could somehow be responsible for the sudden shift in Sophia's feelings towards him.

Seeing the look of dismay on his friend's face as he stared into the distance deep in thought, Robert said he would start looking more deeply into Vincent's affairs early tomorrow morning. Benjamin thanked him profusely, realising that in the meantime he would be obliged to accept that there was nothing he could do. He had to comply with Sophia's request not to see her again, abandon any thoughts he had about a courtship with her, and try to ignore his breaking heart.

Chapter 28

Sophia Receives a Marriage Proposal

It felt like an eternity to Sophia since she had made the painful decision to distance herself from Lord Willoughby, even though it had only been a week. Believing by now that he would easily find himself a much more suitable romance with someone other than with her, she tried very hard not to wonder if he was already interested in someone else. Lady Rosamund had made it clear, making Sophia believe that she would never look beautiful with such a prominent scar on her face. So much so that the more she thought about it, and what Lady Rosamund had said to her, she feared that Benjamin would have been ridiculed for even considering a courtship with her.

Any proposal for her hand in marriage would surely be considered preposterous by others, thereby affecting his position, possibly even at the Royal Academy. Once the ladies of the ton had taken the opportunity to exert their influence on the opinions of their husbands or sons, or indeed any of the gentlemen connected to them, he may well have become a laughing stock. That she could not have borne.

Although she had initially shunned the idea of finding solace in her painting, especially the development of her style which Benjamin had encouraged, it was inevitable that she would return to it. She lost herself for short periods of time in the brushstrokes and colours she had grown to feel comfortable with and believed she knew well. Even though painting was a constant reminder of their deep conversations about painting and artists and talk about visiting other the exhibitions in the future, she continued.

She recalled with aching heart how Benjamin had spoken to her, listened to her, and looked into her eyes. He had made her heart soften, so that it was easy to imagine it had melted into his.

Such thoughts caused her to put down her brush or stare at the blank wall in front of her as she tried to forget what might well have been, while all the while wishing not to.

The truth of the matter remained. Irrespective of anything else, Lord Benjamin Willoughby had become her dearest friend, whose opinion and guidance she valued greatly, and the only man she now believed she could love. This led her to the realisation that her decision would have far reaching consequences for her. Also, she now felt that by rejecting him, she was suffering yet another bereavement. The loss and pain in her heart was so great that she never wished to endure it again. Consequently, it wasn't unreasonable to consider that she might now remain a childless spinster for the rest of her days. However, she told herself that if her current anguish and loneliness resulted in him having a happy life with the woman he deserved, then her suffering was justified.

She had discovered the book about Albrecht Durer which he had left behind not long after his departure, unsure whether it was a gift for her or a loan. Either way, it touched her heart that he had thought to bring it. Presumably, he had wanted to show her all of the things they had talked about last, and she couldn't stop crying when she opened it to see how beautiful the paintings were. They were exactly as Benjamin had described. She stared at the illustrations, tears running down her face. How was she going to be able to carry on without him? Especially when she recalled how difficult it had been for her to make the decision to leave mourning and allow their friendship to develop. She felt she was back in the same dark place as before. Bereft and lonely.

As she gazed at the book, she knew she ought to return it to him with a note. She should write that it was much too valuable a gift for her to accept, when in fact, she couldn't bear to be parted from it. She pored over the images as she ate her meals and placed the book carefully every night on the table in her bedchamber so that she could look at it again during the night. It seemed to her that it was all she had left of Benjamin.

It was also quickly apparent to those who remained in Sophia's life that she had become increasingly withdrawn as the days went by. This was to the extent that she barely uttered a word, and even when she couldn't avoid responding, she used as few words as possible. The situation was much to the concern of Beatrice and Lady Helena, who were once again at a loss as to how to help her. The only thing they could think of to cause such a change in Sophia was that something had happened between her and the handsome Lord Willoughby. But if he were to return, they felt sure Sophia would, without the shadow of a doubt, revert to her former cheerful self.

But the longer his absence grew, the less likely this seemed. Not only had the light seemed to have disappeared from Sophia, but her townhouse once again became a quiet and dreary place. Sophia hadn't spoken of it to anyone else, not even Lady Helena or Beatrice, but they both assumed there had been a tragic falling out with Lord Willoughby. The other observation, on which they sadly agreed, was that something like that should never have happened.

Lady Helena continued to support her daughter-in-law, trying to let her recover in her own way from whatever ailed her. Lady Helena once again blamed fate for dealing Sophia such a cruel blow, especially at such a young age. However, she found not intervening on this occasion easier said than done, for she became very concerned for Sophia's welfare and the decline in her mood and health. Her daughter-in-law had become wan and listless, as if the spark of life inside her had been extinguished for good this time.

Nevertheless, Lady Helena continued to try her best, attempting from time to time to engage Sophia in conversation and offer comfort, but Sophia refused to be drawn out of herself. She remained lost in her own thoughts. Unbeknown to them all, a clear image of Benjamin the last time she had seen him and sent him away was engraved on her mind's eye. She knew she would never forget the look of sorrow in his eyes when she told him to leave. His stutter had returned. This picture of him was now in danger of replacing all of the good memories she should still have had of him and the precious moments they had shared.

On that particular day, however, the quietness in Sophia's drawing room between her and Lady Helena was interrupted by the arrival of Vincent. He didn't waste any time on greeting either of them properly or, indeed, with pleasantries before he came quickly to the point. He announced quite arrogantly that he required their full attention since he had something of great importance to share with them both. He waited impatiently for Sophia to put down her paint brush and his mother her embroidery, as if they were of no consequence whatsoever, before he was prepared to continue.

Sitting comfortably in the chair nearest to the settee where the two ladies were seated, he revealed for the first time that he had been dealing with Mr Blackwood. Obviously, this didn't come as a surprise to Sophia since their meeting had been held at her own townhouse, without her permission or any invitation to attend the proceedings.

What did come as a surprise was that Vincent appeared to be treating the matter as if she didn't have any prior knowledge of it, which really was most peculiar. It was as though he thought she ought not to be curious about it. His reprimand at the art exhibition when she had politely asked about his visit to Spain came quickly to mind, making her wonder again why he was being so secretive. Her house and money belonged to her. Even though he could expect to have some influence on what she did with them, as her eldest male relative, it surely didn't extend to this? It wasn't even as if he had as yet taken Henry's title, she thought.

Unless, of course, this peculiar behaviour was for Lady Helena's benefit, but when Sophia looked curiously at her mother-in-law, she was unable to deduce anything from her facial expression. She remained fully absorbed in what her son was saying. It seemed that he could still do no wrong in her eyes, whereas Sophia took the view now that Vincent definitely was up to something and was trying to hide his movements.

An image of the way he had been as a boy came back to her then, cheating at the games they had played as children, so that he could always be the winner. Or twisting the facts so that he could hide behind them if he chose to or make them appear to his advantage. She had come to the conclusion by now that her brother-in-law was an inveterate liar and a genuinely bad lot!

Unfortunately, she didn't have any more time to pursue that line of thought, as Vincent was still speaking. ". . . So, with the right investment choices, Mr Blackwood, for whom I have the utmost respect and enormous faith in his capabilities, believes he can salvage your precarious financial situation," he said, smiling benevolently at Sophia, as if his intervention had resulted in a miraculous solution to the problem.

If her heart hadn't been broken by the loss of Benjamin, the news might have brought a glimmer of hope to Sophia that she might not also be facing the dire consequence of being penniless. She was, however, even more stunned when Vincent went one step further and spoke directly to her.

"My dearest, Sophia, I truly know and understand how difficult your life must have been since the loss of my brother. After giving the matter considerable thought, I feel it is my duty to set the matter straight. I am certain that I would have Henry's blessing for what I am going to say next." Without any hesitation whatsoever and continuing in the same matter of fact tone of voice, he said, "Sophia, I would like it if you would do me the honour of becoming my wife."

Vincent's proposal was met with a stunned silence from both Sophia and Lady Helena. Neither of them moved a muscle nor even turned their heads to seek support from a glance at each other. His tone of voice and unapproachable demeanour continued to demand their full attention. Sophia was stunned, having never anticipated anything of this sort happening.

After some long moments of silence, the bemused look on their faces seemed to confuse and somewhat unsettle Vincent, who soon became quite flustered and rather red in the face. His annoyance became visible to Sophia in the way he was glaring at her. In what was then was a somewhat irritated tone of voice, he reiterated that their marriage would simply be his way of fulfilling his duty to take care of her, as her brother-in-law, and also to secure their family's future.

He turned to Lady Helena then and remarked that he was certain she would be delighted by the thought of having a grandchild. He suggested it might be as early as the next year, if all went well, as he was certain it would. He smiled at Sophia then in a way she most certainly didn't like or appreciate. Her flesh began to crawl when she thought of being in her bedchamber alone with him.

To her horror, it appeared as if Vincent's assumptions regarding Lady Helena had been correct, for she was now smiling broadly at both of them. Sophia could feel Vincent silently willing her to accept his proposal. Quite different emotions were, however, running through her. These obviously included how she had secretly wished to marry Benjamin, though she continued to believe her reason for turning him away was the right one. But also, she was reminded that finding another suitor could be impossible due to her scar, even if she had wished to do so. However, before she had met Benjamin and Vincent had returned to their lives, the truth of the matter was, she had never thought of her brother-in-law romantically.

Feeling quite overwhelmed by this time and a little faint, she was far from certain that marrying Vincent would be the right decision. However, being unable to avoid noticing his irritation, presumably because he had expected her to be pleased to receive his proposal if not fall into his arms immediately, she had the presence of mind to stand her ground.

Clearing her throat and managing to give him the tiniest of smiles, she said, "Thank you, Vincent. I am sorry for the delay in my response, but I am feeling quite overwhelmed by your generous offer. Please, could I have a little more time to think about your kind proposal?"

To which Vincent nodded and said that she should take all the time she needed. She suspected that despite his words, his intention would be to pressure her for an acceptance at the earliest opportunity. Preferably when they were alone and there wasn't any chance of his mother trying to interfere if Sophia decided to refuse.

She left the room with her thoughts in turmoil, wondering what on earth she had done to deserve all this, and how she could possibly escape the trap she had been caught in.

Chapter 29

The Truth Comes to Light

Two days later, the pain he was suffering from Sophia's rejection seemed even worse to Benjamin. The hope, which had sustained him initially when she didn't return his art book to him, had gradually begun to fade as the hours went by and she did not even try to contact him by letter. He had been undecided whether to leave the book behind but knew at the same time that he wouldn't be able to bear looking at it again, or even have it in the house. If she did return it, he intended to give it to a charity to auction and allow them to use the funds however they chose to help the poor and needy. That way, he reasoned, at least some good could be gained from the sorry situation.

Irrespective of that, he had given it to Sophia and hoped she had decided to keep it for that reason. In his own way it had been an expression of his love for her, his desire to guide and care for her. Even if she wasn't prepared to see him again, and though he might still not know the reason for it, he nevertheless hoped that she would one day realise his intention. He also hoped she would find Durer's paintings an inspiration for continuing with her own work, or at the very least, to help keep alive her love of great artists and their achievements. There were so many others he had wished to share with her, if only he had had the chance.

Benjamin smiled sadly when he recalled their earlier discussion about William Turner and John Constable. It suddenly came to him that she might have been expecting him to give her a book of love poetry or one of the novels by Miss Jane Austen, which he believed had become popular. But that simply wasn't his way. His thoughts drifted briefly to Elizabeth Bennet and Mr Darcy, of which it had to be said he knew little. He had believed his book about Durer was more suited to them because the passion they shared was for art and she would regard it as a reflection of his love for her.

As much as he tried to focus on his own responsibilities, Sophia's image continued to haunt him at every opportunity. It soon became perfectly clear to him that he couldn't let her go. At least, not without a fight. He remembered again his father's counsel that a gentleman needed to choose his battles wisely, and this had to be the most important one of his life—to win back the heart of the woman whose soul belonged with his own. With this thought uppermost in his mind, his determination to uncover the truth about Vincent Montgomery's intentions grew stronger every minute that Sophia and he were apart. He feared more than ever for her safety in the hands of such a rogue as the man clearly was.

What Benjamin didn't realise was that fate also had its own hand to play in this battle, and that his aunt would continue to be a willing participant in helping him win back Sophia's affections. Whilst her nephew walked endlessly backwards and forwards across his study, consumed by the urgent fire within him to do something to resolve his predicament, Lady Margaret arrived unexpectedly to see him. Benjamin, though not feeling like entering into conversation with anyone, made his way to the drawing room with his head bent low. Lady Margaret's heart went out to him as soon as she saw the broken man standing in front of her. Without waiting for him to formally greet her, she made her way to him.

Reaching for his hand, she said, "Benjamin, look at me! I have something important I must say to you." He looked at her listlessly as she went on.

"I overheard your mother talking to one of her friends at the garden tea party I attended yesterday. I quite clearly heard her say that she had called on Sophia, with the sole intention of putting her firmly in her place. She said she told her outright that a scarred widow such as her had absolutely no right to pursue your hand in marriage, or any other gentleman's hand, for that matter. Benjamin, it was despicable behaviour on her part and simply cannot be allowed to stand! I am repeating her words exactly as she said them to her friend," she assured him, clearly appalled by lady Rosamund's actions.

The old lady continued venting her spleen. "It isn't difficult to imagine what she actually said to Sophia, and it saddens me even

160

more to tell you that your mother appears to have done this without any qualms whatsoever. She had no consideration for the misery and damage her actions might cause. Instead, she clearly felt it was her right and duty to inflict such vicious nonsense on that poor young woman. She thinks she is justified, doing it in her capacity as your mother."

Even before Lady Margaret finished speaking, Benjamin realised that his mother's interference was the reason behind Sophia's rejection of him. Even without his aunt repeating the conversation she had overheard in full, he had guessed it instantly when she told him that his mother had taken the liberty of calling on Sophia. He was furious with his mother, of course, but at the same time, hope flickered in his heart. All was not lost after all! There was some hope that they could be reconciled. If Sophia would only allow him to speak to her again, he could try to persuade her to excuse his mother's appalling behaviour. As for his feelings towards Lady Rosamund, it really was the final straw. He didn't even know at that point whether he wished to have anything more to do with her.

Benjamin thanked his aunt profusely, and, seeing the look of concern on her face, he assured her that she had done the right thing in coming to tell him. She took her leave shortly afterwards. While Benjamin was thinking about what he might say to Sophia in a letter asking if he might call on her again, the butler announced the arrival of his best friend.

Soames said that Mr Robert apparently wished to speak to him urgently. Though still somewhat flustered, Benjamin welcomed Robert into the study, where his friend came quickly to the point. He revealed that he had discovered Vincent Montgomery was definitely up to no good. He told Benjamin that, in the end, not being able to find out anything else of value from his other friends and business associates, Robert had hired a private investigator whom he knew to be discreet. He had looked into Vincent's activities. As Robert continued with his explanation,

161

Benjamin began to clench his fists, unable any longer to contain his anger.

It appeared that Vincent and Sophia's lawyer had been colluding together, with the intention of cheating her out of the considerable sum of money, and the bulk of the estate she had inherited from her late husband. They reasoned that she was unlikely to be aware of the extent of her inheritance as Mr Blackwood had full control of the funds, to which, it turned out, he had been helping himself whenever he liked. Robert further revealed that the only way for Vincent to properly access Sophia's wealth would be through marriage. The pair of them had obviously realised if she had consented to accept your hand in marriage, the control would pass to her new husband. You!

"I'm afraid that the situation is even more serious than that, Benjamin. My investigator's source knows of a number of conversations between the lawyer and Vincent Montgomery. She also said that Vincent visited his brother Henry at his house on the night of the fire. They argued when he tried again to extort money from his brother, and it came to blows. Somehow, a lamp was knocked dover and that was how the fire started. Vincent got out of the house unharmed, but presumably not wishing to be implicated in any wrongdoing, he didn't raise the alarm. Apparently, he had knocked Henry out . . . and left him there to die."

A stunned silence followed as both men attempted to come to terms with the horrible tale. Finally, Benjamin asked how the investigator knew all of this.

"I think you have probably realised by this time that Vincent enjoys drinking too much and not always in the most respectable of company. A young woman with whom he had been associating at one of the less desirable inns on the docks told my investigator what she knew for a small sum of money. It seems that Vincent was quite taken by her charms, and since she was clearly of a similar ilk to himself, could easily be bribed to reveal what he had told her. He had apparently called it his grand plan to make them both rich. He had tempted her with all of the furs and jewels she could have once he had the money, which he claimed was rightly his as the eldest son. He professed in his cups to hate his sister-in-law, Sophia, since she was somehow at the root of it, and he would be glad to see her destitute.

"His plan is to take Henry's title, marry Sophia as soon as he can, in a quiet ceremony without any guests, and disappear abroad with the family fortune, including his mother's money. He plans to leave the two women destitute. And there's more, I'm afraid. Vincent hatched this plan with Mr Blackwood immediately after Henry's death, and they have both been receiving regular payments of small amounts from Sophia's fortune. The lawyer was certain they wouldn't be noticed if she had someone independent look through the ledgers on her behalf. This situation is apparently to continue until Vincent marries her, when Mr Blackwood can expect to receive a more substantial sum for his assistance."

Benjamin, in shock now, slumped in his chair in disbelief as Robert went on.

"Lord Francis Sudley, another of my friends whom you may not have met, owed me a favour, so he also spoke to Mr Blackwood, whom he knew something of. At the same time as offering him a substantial bribe, he plied the lawyer on our behalf with an excess of food and wine. He listened to the lawyer boasting in his cups about the influence he has. Until Francis turned the conversation to Vincent Montgomery, whom he said he regarded as a close friend. The lawyer boasted then that he had helped Vincent pass some of the information he had acquired from another source onto the French. He believed that this had had a direct effect on the outcome of Napoleonic war. Francis had already heard rumours about Vincent spying for Napoleon, so he wasn't surprised. Vincent had been seen drinking with Nelson's officers, from whom he might well have learned their plans, which he would have had no qualms whatsoever in selling to the French.

"Well, as you can imagine, Francis was understandably disgusted by that, and he wished to ensure that Mr Blackwood's actions in assisting Vincent not only come to light but that both he and the lawyer should also receive the punishment they deserve. So, he was more than glad to reveal to me what he had discovered."

Benjamin realised straight away that the news could easily have been the reason Vincent had reprimanded Sophia so sharply at the exhibition when she had asked when he had been in Spain. Clearly, he had wished to keep his whereabouts a secret, for he had likely at the time been abroad. That was undoubtedly because he had no desire to face a charge of treason and end up at the end of the hangman's rope, Benjamin concluded. A man like Vincent Montgomery would have obviously made a lot of enemies, and it wasn't unreasonable to consider that he might well have continued to try to hide his whereabouts and movements by not staying in one place for very long.

"Benjamin, there is no doubt in my mind whatsoever that Vincent Montgomery is a villain! Those who know him, or of him, don't have a good word to say about his reputation and character," Robert said urgently, looking with concern at his friend before adding, "Now, you need to decide quickly how you are going to use this knowledge to help Lady Sophia."

Despite his shock at the sudden turn of events, Benjamin decided quickly. He thanked Robert for his help, then he wasted no time in instructing his butler to have his horse saddled immediately. He refusing Robert's kind offer to accompany him, telling him that this was something he must do alone. Irrespective of their falling out, Sophia was in danger from her brother-in-law, who appeared prepared to stop at nothing to get what he wanted, including murder and treason. It was something which he had to deal with alone.

A short while later, Benjamin's heart was racing as he approached Sophia's townhouse, determined to put an end to all this skullduggery and regain her love, which he believed now was rightly his.

Chapter 30

Love Conquers All

Meanwhile, Sophia was sitting in her drawing room with Lady Helena and Vincent. Given how anxious she felt about what she was about to do, her whole body trembled and her stomach churned. She had asked them both to come so that she could inform them of her decision regarding Vincent's marriage proposal together. Not being able to see any way forward with her own life now that she had lost Benjamin, she reasoned that marrying Vincent would at least be a way of repaying Lady Helena for her considerable kindness. She firmly believed her mother-in-law would be delighted if she married Henry's brother and the Montgomery family became whole again.

Nevertheless, as she announced her decision, Sophia couldn't help but feel overwhelmed by an intense feeling of loss. She tried hard not to cry, but her heart ached for the connection she had shared with Benjamin. She so desperately wanted to see him again and explain everything that was happening to her. But she knew it would not come to pass.

And now, Vincent was smiling warmly at her, assuring her that she had made the right decision. At that moment, however, they were all suddenly rudely interrupted by the drawing room door bursting open. To her shock, on the threshold stood a very determined looking Benjamin. His eyes met Sophia's, and she saw the intensity of the fire burning within him.

"To what do we owe the honour of your ill-mannered intrusion on this occasion, Lord Willoughby?" Vincent said, his voice laced with sarcasm. Benjamin's gaze remained fixed on Sophia as he ignored his adversary.

166

Speaking directly and only to her, he said gently, "I have just discovered the most likely reason why you rejected me, Sophia. My mother was wrong to say what I imagine she said. Sadly, I know only too well how badly she can behave. I also couldn't help but overhear you accepting this man's proposal as I came through the door." He stared at Vincent in disgust. "I will refrain from calling him a gentleman because he most certainly isn't that! Whether or not you consent to see me again, which I sincerely hope you will, it's imperative that you don't marry him. Sophia, please believe me when I tell you that I have evidence to prove Vincent Montgomery has been deceiving both you and Lady Helena all along. He is guilty of the worst possible crimes, along with your lawyer Mr Blackwood."

For Sophia, the sudden shift in Vincent's demeanour confirmed the truth of Benjamin's words. As she looked from him to her brother-in-law, she also knew it in her heart. Benjamin had come here today to help and protect her.

In a fit of rage, recognising that he had too much to lose if his affairs became known to the authorities, Vincent pushed past Benjamin and hastily left the drawing room. He slammed the front door of the townhouse behind him. Lady Helena, who hid her distress well, also quickly left the room. That gave Benjamin and Sophia a moment alone, without a chaperone, something which, if her intuition served her well, wouldn't matter in the least despite what was about to occur.

Sophia and Benjamin stared into each other's eyes as he proclaimed his love for her in a voice filled with raw emotion and pulled her gently, willingly, into his arms. When he let her go, it was only so that he could fall onto one knee and ask her if she would do him the honour of becoming his wife.

Sophia was overwhelmed by the look in his eyes. Lord Benjamin Willoughby really did love her! So much so that she could no longer hold back her own feelings. With her eyes brimming with tenderness, she confessed her love for him, telling him that she would be overjoyed to accept his proposal.

Benjamin pulled her to him again, so that they might share the sweetest of kisses. It was one which lingered in both of their hearts for a lifetime.

"I have been so unhappy without you, my dearest Sophia," he said a little later, with his arms still around her. "I don't feel as if I could go through being apart from you again."

With her eyes misted in tears of happiness, she whispered, "Love is fragile at the best of times, Benjamin. I should never have sent you away. I'm truly sorry. After what your mother said, I made the wrong decision. I believed I could live without you when I can't. Irrespective of whether or not I have a scar on my face."

He answered her without having to think about it. "My mother had absolutely no right to come between us! Wishing to marry you was always my choice. It was not hers to make for me, but you'll come to see that, sadly, she doesn't listen to a word I say." Benjamin smiled. "I love you, Sophia Montgomery, and that's all that matters. Also, of course, that you have consented now to be my wife."

Benjamin's lips sought hers again in a kiss which deepened as the strength and power of true love coursed through them. This time, they would not be parted.

Epilogue

A few weeks later when Sophia married Benjamin in a quiet ceremony, she was wearing a stunning green dress, which she loved which everyone admired. It had been made from the fabric she had chosen when she had visited the modiste's shop with Beatrice, on a day that now seemed like a very long time ago.

So much of her life had changed since then and would change irrevocably for the better that day. She couldn't believe how happy she felt as she laughed and giggled with a delighted Lizzie, who helped her get dressed that morning. The maid had also excelled herself in how expertly she had arranged her ladyship's hair, using several pink rosebuds which the flower seller had delivered earlier that morning. Sophia was delighted at her appearance as she stared in wonder at her reflection in the looking glass. She did not even notice her scar, for she thought she looked beautiful, as Benjamin always told her she was.

He had told her that she must try to stop thinking about it. It only made her unhappy. Moreover, he insisted, he had fallen in love with her, so every part of her had grown very dear to him. This conversation and his quiet insistence had helped Sophia to change her view of the matter. She now focused on other areas of her appearance, having made many more visits to the modiste's shop with Beatrice and Lady Helena, to order her wedding dress and a whole new wardrobe. That was fitting for a newly married woman, and it was much to Lizzie's delight. The maid clearly loved all the new the gowns, bonnets, and shoes as much as Sophia did.

Sophia gave away or discarded many of the clothes she already had, especially her mourning dresses. Lizzie had been overcome by the sheer number of clothes Sophia had passed on to her when she cleared out her wardrobe, and she had already started to alter them so they would fit her and her family.

However, Sophia still kept the pale blue dress she had worn early in her relationship with Benjamin and the purple dress she always wore when she painted. Both had a special place in her heart.

She hugged Lizzie when she was at last dressed in all her wedding finery and took a final glance at herself in the looking glass. She thanked her maid profusely for how beautiful she had made her look, but also for the many ways in which her faithful maid had helped to support her during her darkest hours. Lizzie cried when Sophia gave her a silver bracelet which, even though she said was far too good for her, she put on immediately. She swore it was the nicest thing anyone had ever given to her as a gift and that she would never take it off.

Only the couple's closest friends and family were invited to attend the ceremony. Beatrice's face was filled with joy as she walked behind Sophia as her maid of honour, to the altar where Benjamin was waiting for her best friend. Robert stood proudly next to him as his best man. Lady Rosamund was also there on the arm of her eldest son Simon. Having admitted her wrongdoing, she had begged Benjamin for his forgiveness and received it.

She had also made an apology of sorts to Sophia, which, it had to be said, she had found difficult to do. Seeing how happy Benjamin seemed with Sophia had over time made her realise all the more how wrong she had been in trying to match him with Lady Charlotte Sinclair.

Lady Margaret had called on her sister-in-law after the news of her nephew's proposal to Sophia had died down. She had wanted to give her time to become more used to the thought of them marrying, however much she still disliked the idea. Until then, Lady Rosamund had remained distant, barely speaking to Benjamin unless she absolutely needed to. It caused Benjamin much unhappiness, even though he had fully expected it, but he had decided she must come around in her own time.

So it was that Sophia found herself confronted one day by Lady Rosamund, who admitted quite plainly that her behaviour had been abhorrent and inexcusable. It was not, she said, at all how a mother should behave, especially not to such a dear and kind-hearted young man as Benjamin. She confessed she had effectively pushed him into making a choice between the woman he clearly adored, Sophia, and his own mother. She was, she said, utterly reprehensible!

In due course, it seemed that Lady Rosamund had once more gritted her teeth and sent a letter to Benjamin to ask if he would be prepared to see her privately. His response was immediate; he would come to her townhouse at the time she had suggested. He knew that by visiting her he would be able leave whenever he chose should she become too aggravated during their conversation. Of course, after she apologised, he forgave her instantly, hating being at odds with her.

Meanwhile, Sophia had also prepared to forgive her future mother-in-law, mostly for Benjamin's sake, hoping they might one day become friends. She also very much wished for Lady Rosamund to attend the wedding ceremony. She loved Benjamin far too much not to do anything for him to make him happy, and she knew that he didn't like falling out with anyone, least of all his own mother.

After she had accepted his proposal, she dreamed that she heard Henry's voice calling her name and thought she glimpsed his face. He was telling her to be happy. She had awoken with tears on her cheeks, knowing that she had to do as he said and seize the moment. It wasn't a betrayal. Henry was gone. Not because he had wished to leave her but because of the hand fate had dealt him.

As Benjamin was making his marriage vows to her, she thought again of how she would always regard him as the man with the kindest eyes and heart. She smiled to realise that she couldn't have done anything else other than fall in love with him. Her heart soared when the vicar pronounced them man and wife, and they shared a gentle kiss before the approving congregation. She did not think she could ever be happier!

Benjamin didn't once doubt that he had made the right decision in proposing to Sophia, especially when he was standing next to her before the altar. He had given his heart to her in a way he didn't think he could have done anyone else. Certainly not Lady

Sinclair! He felt the same confidence when talking to Sophia as he did his aunt, for his stutter quite disappeared. It seemed to him to be the most natural thing in the world to be at Sophia's side and for her to become his wife.

After the ceremony, the newlyweds and their guests gathered at the wedding breakfast, hosted by both Lady Margaret and Rosamund. The pair had decided that they also needed to make their peace with each other, for the sake of the love they shared for Benjamin and his late father.

A little later in the evening, after a splendid feast, Benjamin and Sophia stepped onto the dance floor for their first waltz as husband and wife. As the music came to an end, they shared the tenderest of kisses, sealing their commitment to a lifetime of happiness with each other.

Extended Epilogue

It transpired later that Vincent was nowhere to be found. He had left London, presumably afraid that Benjamin was about to reveal the extent of his deceit and treachery. It seemed unlikely that he would be back since it would mean facing the consequences of his criminal activities. It would likely result in him being sentenced to hang for treason. Mr. Blackwood had already met his fate. The lawyer hadn't been as quick to leave the city as his partner in crime. After Robert and Benjamin had spoken to the authorities, he had been arrested and was now confined to prison to await trial.

Justice had prevailed, but Cupid was given the final word on the matter. Sophia and Benjamin's love for each other continued to grow stronger with each passing day. Two years after their wedding, they were blessed with the birth of a daughter, and not long afterwards, they eagerly anticipated the arrival of their second child.

Sophia continued to pursue her art, much to her husband's pleasure and delight. Working with a passion which matched his own, her skills continued to develop. With his ongoing encouragement and support, she looked forward to holding a small exhibition of her work. It was to include her painting of the rose which Benjamin had admired the first time he saw it. He still cherished it, saying it was one of his favourite paintings.

He had also managed to buy the landscape painting by the unknown artist which Sophia had been viewing at the Royal Academy when he saw her for the first time. To her delight, he had presented it to her on her birthday after their marriage, and it now had pride of place in their drawing room. Every time Sophia looked at it, she knew it would forever be a symbol of their love and all they had endured to be together. For that reason alone, she treasured it.

Benjamin had told her that he wished to take her on a tour of Europe once their children were a little older, of course, and might be left with their grandparents. Or even later on if she didn't wish to leave them behind. In the meantime, they could console themselves very happily with the thought that there was a wealth of art in the British Isles for them still to discover. The current lack of opportunity for them to travel for practical reasons was of little consequence, they agreed, when they had each other.

The Ladies Helena and Rosamund had soon become doting grandmothers. Beatrice's daughter had also formed a close friendship with Sophia and Benjamins's little girl Suzanna. Even Lady Charlotte Sinclair had found happiness in marrying the marquess she loved not long after Benjamin and Sophia's engagement had been announced. Gossip said the couple were expecting their first child, with great excitement.

With Benjamin's support, Sophia had recently revealed to Lady Helena what she had failed to convey earlier concerning Henry's poor opinion of Vincent's lack of standards. She explained that she had not wished to hurt her mother-in-law fat the time, but she had since realised that she should have voiced her concern at the outset about Vincent's reputation. Lady Helena did not seem surprised to hear that Vincent had asked Henry on several occasions for money to pay his creditors.

In return, Lady Helena had told Sophia that, in Henry's absence, she would always be grateful to Benjamin for coming to their assistance. She knew he had saved them both from a miserable life with Vincent, even possibly being abandoned to a state of penury on the streets! She confessed she had developed the highest regard for Lord Benjamin Willoughby, his quiet and gentle manner, and the acts of kindness he did wherever he went. She admitted she dearly wished she could have said the same about her eldest son.

When Sophia relayed this to Benjamin, she pointed out that it was not just her who thought he was entirely wonderful. He smiled when she stroked his face and called him her hero, adding that he was the best husband and best Papa in the world. The, he kissed her passionately and told her that it was all because of her and the love she had brought into his gloomy life. Sophia sighed happily, resting in his arms. After all she had been through, she now knew with absolute certainty that it was possible to have a second chance at love, and to find true, everlasting happiness.

The End

Printed in Great Britain
by Amazon

36292916R00097